The Little One

Jayne Osborne

Published in 2024 by FeedARead.com Publishing

A CIP catalogue record for this title is available from the British Library.

For Christine and Anne. In their own ways they both gave me the courage to go ahead with this.

Chapter One

The office door opened to allow a gust of cold wind inside, and Deborah huddled closer into her jumper. It was cold inside the office, for there didn't appear to be any heating, and every time the door opened, she got even colder. "Can I help you?" she asked, and the man who had entered looked at her. She was small, very thin, dressed in old but neat clothes, and her hair which was long and blonde, was pulled back into a pony tail. Her eyes were deep blue, and she had an air about her which made her look very old, much older than she actually was. "Hello," he said, "Are you Anne?" she shook her head. "No, I'm Deborah Parkes. How may I help you?" The man smiled at her. "Oh, sorry, I was mistaken. I've got an appointment with Mr. Cummins" he said now, "the name is Hayden Tomlinson. Can you tell him I'm here please"

"Certainly" she said, "please take a seat, and I'll let him know." She got up then, and walked to the office door, knocked and opened it. "Mr. Tomlinson is here to see you Mr. Cummins" she said, and the man inside the office looked up. "Show him in" he said, and Deborah went back to the outer office. "Mr. Cummins will see you now" she said, and ushered him past her, into the office, before going back to her desk. She thought about the visitor, as she looked at her shorthand notebook again, found her place and started to type, wondering what the man wanted her uncle to do. He was tall, had hair that was the just a bit darker than hers, but he didn't appear to be very old, mid- thirties perhaps, and he had deep brown eyes that seemed to see everything. He was powerfully built as well, but

he'd looked friendly. Her thoughts were interrupted by the office door opening. "Deborah" her boss called. "Make coffee" and the door shut again. Deborah went to the cloakroom to fill the kettle, and started to make the coffee. When it was ready, she put everything onto the tray, and knocked on the office door, before opening it and taking the tray inside. She was surprised when it was taken from her by the visitor, and she smiled her thanks at him. "We're going to be busy for a while Deborah" her boss said, "but Mr. Tomlinson will be having dinner with me tonight. When you get home, make sure that your aunt knows that he's coming."
"Very well Mr. Cummins. Will it be okay if I go on time?" she asked. "Aunt will expect me home, and if you're going to be late, she'll need to know."
"Yes, yes, go at 5.00, but make sure you bring the letters in before you go." he said. "Now go and finish your work. I'll post the letters on the way home."
Deborah went back to her desk. Oh great, she thought, he was going to come to dinner tonight. That meant she'd have to go without again, for her aunt only ever bought enough food for the three of them, and if her uncle asked somebody to dine, then she had to go without. Their son seemed to take delight in visiting his parents unannounced, and taking her portion of the meal, but that was typical of her cousin Dudley. He was almost ten years older than her, was also her uncles' solicitor, and had told her aunt and uncle that she would cost them a lot after her parents had died, and delighted in making things difficult for her. He had collaborated with her uncle in taking control of everything after her father had died, and she knew

they were cheating her, but there seemed to be nothing she could do about it. He was solidly built as well, and had inherited her uncles' strong left hand, which she had experienced on a few occasions especially when she had asked for some money. She sighed, and got on with the typing. All the letters and their envelopes were laid into a folder, which her uncle would sign, if he left the office after she did. When 5.00 came around, she took the letters into her uncle's office and laid them on the desk and got his permission to leave, before she put her coat on, and prepared to leave the office.

She walked quickly back to the house where she and her parents had lived and which her aunt and uncle had appropriated, and opened the door with her key. "Is that you Deborah?" her aunt called, and she went into the sitting room, where her aunt was laying on a sofa in front of the gas fire. She was a large woman, made even larger by the chocolates and sweets she ate every day, and the fact that she never did any exercise at all, apart from going shopping once a day. "Yes, Aunt Claudia" she said quietly.
"You're late" snapped her aunt, but Deborah knew she wasn't. "Sorry Aunty." she said quietly. "I had to finish some letters for Uncle. He asked me to tell you that he's entertaining a client tonight, and will be bringing him home for dinner."
"Very well" her aunt said coldly. "You'd better go and start on the dinner then. It's pork chops, and vegetables. I've put out the vegetables on the kitchen table. Don't overcook the pork will you" she said as she lay back against the cushions. "You can make an

apple crumble for dessert, and there's some cream in the fridge." Deborah knew there was no use in asking her aunt if she had done any preparation for dinner, but said nothing as she turned away and went out of the sitting room, removing her coat as she did so, and going upstairs to hang it in the small room she had had ever since her father had died, and her aunt and uncle had moved in. She tidied her hair, then went downstairs again, this time going into the kitchen. The breakfast dishes hadn't been washed, and that was her first job, before she could clear enough space to start on the dinner preparation. She had the dishes washed, she'd put the vacuum cleaner over the floor in the dining room, the vegetables were prepared, and the chops seasoned, ready for cooking, when she heard the front door open, and knew her uncle was home with the visitor, and finished chopping the apples for the dessert hurriedly. Her aunt called her from the sitting room, and she went in. The visitor was sitting in the easy chair by the fire, and her uncle was standing warming himself in front of it. He was a tall, overweight man, dressed in his usual smart suit, but his belly was protruding over his waistband, and he glared at her as she entered. "Get us some drinks" he ordered. "Your Aunt and I will have our usual, and Mr. Tomlinson will have a Whisky" She went out without speaking, and went to get the drinks from the cabinet in the dining room. She poured the drinks, took them back into the sitting room and handed them around, before she went back into the kitchen again, and started to cook the dinner. She had laid the table in the dining room for the meal, and put the vegetables into their dishes, put the chops on the plates, and put everything on the table, after telling them that the meal was ready. When she heard the bell ringing, she went into the dining room, cleared away the plates from the main course, and took the dessert in, before going back to the kitchen. Hayden Tomlinson looked at his host and hostess. “Doesn't your niece eat with you?” he asked. Her uncle shook his head. “Certainly not” he said, his voice shocked. “She eats in the kitchen when we have a guest.”

“But she's your secretary as well?” Hayden asked, and her uncle nodded. “She works for me yes” he answered. “We bought her up after her father died, but she likes cooking, so she insists on doing all the cooking, and she offered to do my secretarial work, so she pays back her debt that way.”

“Her debt?” Hayden asked, and her uncle tried to laugh. His wife said hurriedly, “She feels that she owes us for having bought her up after her father died, so she insists that she pays us back.” Deborah had eaten a small meal of vegetables, for she hadn't dared take too much, and hoped there would be some of the apple crumble left, for she had always liked that. She was still hungry, when she heard the bell ring and went to clear away the remains of the meal. As usual, there was no dessert left, and she knew her uncle had eaten more than his fair share, so she would have to go without. She had made the coffee, taken it into the sitting room and put it on the table in front of her aunt, before leaving the room again. Hayden took the cup of coffee offered to him by her uncle, and her aunt sat to one side, as they discussed the work Hayden wanted done. They finished their discussion, and Hayden stood to take his leave. “Might I go and say thank you

to your niece for cooking the dinner?" he asked, but her aunt shook her head. "I don't think she'd like that" she said. "I'll pass on you thanks to her."
Hayden nodded. "Thank you for your hospitality" he said, "and please pass my thanks on to your niece for her cooking. The food was delicious" Mr. Cummins escorted him to the door, and he took his leave. Deborah was standing by the door, listening to the guest leaving, and drew in a deep breath. She had cleared up the kitchen, and left it in order for the morning, and wanted to go to bed, but couldn't leave the kitchen, until her aunt or uncle came in to inspect it, and make sure that it was in order for her to do so. Her uncle came into the kitchen, and inspected everything. "You can go to bed" he said. "I'll be out of the office until 10.00 tomorrow morning. Make sure you're there on time." and he stalked out of the room. Deborah drew in another deep breath, thankful that he seemed to be in a good mood and hadn't found fault with anything in the kitchen, and made her way up to bed. The room was cold, for the heating wasn't turned on in it, and she wasted no time in getting into bed, made sure her alarm clock was set, laid down, and was soon asleep.

The following morning, she got ready for the day ahead and made her way downstairs and set the table in the dining room, before putting some water on to boil. She could hear her uncle moving around, and put the bacon ready to cook, and the bread to put into the toaster. He put his head round the door, and glared at her. "Take your aunt a cup of tea" he ordered, "and then I'll have mine with my breakfast. Don't break the egg, like you did yesterday" and he was gone again. Deborah poured the drink, and took a cup into her aunt's bedroom. She pulled the curtains after she had put the cup down on the bedside table, and her aunt glared at her. "You're late" she spat at her, but Deborah didn't answer back. "Good morning, Aunt Claudia" she said. "I'm just going to cook uncle his breakfast." and was gone before the older woman could say anything. She opened the fridge door and looked inside. She was still hungry after last night's light meal, but as usual there was nothing in it, but a few slices of bread, and her uncles ration of eggs and bacon, and she hurriedly ate some bread as she cooked her uncles' breakfast. She was careful not to break the egg yolk, and placed the meal in front of him. "You can go and get my toast" he ordered, and she went back to the kitchen, where she toasted some bread and took it into the dining room. Her own meal of toast was soon eaten, and she went back into the dining room to remove the dirty plates. "I've got to leave now uncle" she said, and he nodded.

When she reached the office, she had opened up, and got on with the work left from the day before, and she was typing fast, when the door opened, and Hayden Tomlinson walked in. "Hello" he said, "Is your uncle in?"
"No, sorry" she replied and smiled at him. "He won't be in until about 10.00. Would you like to come back then?"
"Would I be able to wait for him?" he asked, and she nodded. "Would you like a coffee?" she said, and when he nodded, went to make the drink. When it

was ready, she bought him a cup, and handed it to him. "Aren't you going to have any?" he asked, but she shook her head. "It's not time for me to have my drink yet" she replied. "I'm sorry, I can't offer any biscuits, Uncle has locked them away, and I don't have the key." He smiled, then frowned as he processed what she had said.

"I'm sorry, did you say he's locked them away?" Deborah nodded. "He likes to make sure that he has control over the food" she muttered "so, he locks the cupboard where they're kept, and it's only unlocked when he's here." Hayden didn't answer that, he was a bit gobsmacked to be honest. "I want to thank you for cooking such a delicious meal last night" he said, "I wanted to thank you last night, but your aunt said you wouldn't like it."

"Thank you" she smiled. "I'm glad you enjoyed it."

"I was a bit surprised when you didn't eat with us" he said, but she shook her head. "Aunt and Uncle don't like me eating with them when they have guests" she replied, but didn't say anything else, and there was silence in the room, before she spoke again. "Would you object if I got on with my work?" she asked. "I've got quite a bit to do before Uncle gets here, and dictates a load more."

"I don't mind" he said, "I'll sit here and wait for your uncle." She nodded, walked back to her desk, and got on with the work that she hadn't been able to finish the night before. She was busy typing the last few invoices, when the office door opened, and her uncle walked in. He didn't see Hayden Tomlinson sitting behind the screen that separated the door from the body of the office, and sniffed the air. "You've been making coffee again" he thundered at Deborah, "It's not time for you to have coffee yet. Did you think you could get away with having a sly cup while I wasn't here?" He came towards her, his hand raised as if to strike, but a voice behind him stopped him in his tracks. "I'm sorry, Mr. Cummins, it was my fault. I arrived early to see you, and Deborah kindly offered me coffee while I waited." Her uncle dropped his hand immediately, and turned to greet his guest with a smile on his face. "Oh, good morning, Mr. Tomlinson. Sorry *I* wasn't here to meet you. Won't you come into the office? Would you like more coffee?" Hayden shook his head, his thoughts racing, as he thought back to the scene he had just interrupted. "No, thank you. Deborah looked after me very well. Thank you, Deborah, I'm grateful for the drink." He followed the older man into the office, and closed the door behind him. Deborah sat where she was, grateful that he had spoken up, for her uncle was quite capable of striking her. She yawned, as she got on with her work, sorted out the post that had arrived earlier, and when she heard the office door open, she was able to smile at Hayden as he left after shaking hands with her uncle. "Goodbye Deborah" he said, "nice to have met you." and he left the office. Deborah stared after him, and thought how pleasant he had been. Her smile faded, as her uncle grabbed the pile of post from the desk. "Come and take dictation" he ordered, and wearily, she got up, picked up her notebook and pencils, and followed her uncle into the office.

Hayden Tomlinson slowed his stride as he left the office and thought back to the scene he had witnessed.

It had seemed that her uncle was going to strike her, just for making coffee, and what had she said, that it wasn't time for her to have a cup yet? He frowned at that comment, and went into the cafe along the road, from the offices to think. The cafe was empty, and he sat down at a table near the counter. He ordered a drink and a snack he didn't really want, and sat to think about things. He had gone to see Mr. Cummins, for the building firm was well known throughout the district, and although the prices he had been quoted for the work that needed doing on his grandmother's house were fair, he wasn't ready yet to make a decision, but his grandmother had insisted on him using the firm, for she had used them in the past, and got on well with the owner. But when they had been speaking the night before, he had told her that Mr. Parkes had died, and she had remarked that the building firm should have gone to Deborah. He shook his head again, and wondered why she was working as a secretary when she owned the firm. The waitress bought him his drink and a teacake, and he thanked her. “I've just been to see Mr. Cummins” he said, chattily, “No offer of anything to eat, and I just fancy a quick snack” The girl snorted. “Oh him,” she said. “Not well liked round these parts. Of course, when his brother-in-law ran the place, it was much better.”

“His brother-in-law?” he asked, and the girl smiled. “Oh, he was a lovely man. He would always get his catering done by us, when he had visitors. Now, you're lucky if you can get a biscuit from the new owner. When Mr. Parkes was alive, if he had visitors, then his secretary would ring us, and we'd take sandwiches and cakes down. That stopped when he died.”

“Was that long ago?” he asked, but the girl shook her head. “About three or four years ago. His secretary, Anne, was really upset. She'd been there years, and she was very upset when she had to leave.”
“Anne?” he queried, “His secretary is called Deborah and she's still there.”
“She's not a paid secretary,” the girl said, “she's old Cummins niece. Deborah is Mr. Parkes daughter. Anne Stewart was given the sack, no notice or anything, when Mr. Cummins took over the business.”
“So, why didn't Deborah take over the business, if she was Mr. Parkes daughter?”
“Well, there was something odd there. We did hear that her father had left her the business, but her uncle took it from her. She has to work there now. We see her sometimes, and she looks awful. She's lost so much weight since he died and she never seems to have any new clothes. She would come in here to have her lunch with her father, when he was working, but we haven't seen her in here since her uncle took over.”
He nodded, and the girl went back to working behind the counter. He ate the cake and drank the coffee, and pushed the cup away, He stood up and went to the counter, to pay for his meal, and the girl smiled at him. “If you see Deborah again” she said quietly, “can you tell her that Susie from the cafe says hello.”
“Can't you go and tell her yourself?” he asked, but she shook her head. “We're not allowed in the offices at all.” she said quietly. “Her uncle doesn't like her talking to other people. The last time I saw her, I smiled and said hello, and he was with her, and he grabbed her arm, and pulled her away, so she couldn't talk.”
“I might be going to see him again” Hayden said, “I'll

try and pass on your message."
"Thanks" she took his money, and he left the cafe, which was starting to fill up with people now that the lunch break was approaching.

"You can go and get some stamps" Deborah's uncle said, reaching into the petty cash tin, that was bulging with notes. "We need 50 first class." He reached for the calculator and worked out how much it was, and gave her the exact amount. "Don't take all day about it, either. I'm going out to lunch, so be back here by 12.30 otherwise there'll be trouble." She nodded, and went to get her coat, and ran along the road to the post office. There was a queue at that time of day, and she was racing back along the road, to be back on time, when Hayden saw her again. "Deborah" he called, and she skidded to a halt. "Deborah, I wanted to talk to you" he said urgently but she shook her head. "Sorry, I've got to be back in the office by 12.30. Uncle is going out, and told me not to be late." He nodded, "Okay, I'll see you." he said, and watched as she ran back to the office. Her uncle was waiting for her, looking at his watch. "You're late" he said, as she opened the door, and raised his hand. The blow on the side of her head, caught her unawares, and she fell sideways and hit her head on the door frame as she went down. "Serves you right" her uncle said, took the stamps from her, told her to get on with her work, and left the office.

Hayden had dealt with the most urgent of his grandmother's requests, and was now free to go back to her house. He was not due to start work at the local hospital, for another four weeks, and his mother had asked him to keep an eye on the old lady. He decided he would go and pass on Susie's message to Deborah, as her uncle was going out, and she should be alone in the office. He made his way to the office, and went in. Deborah was sitting at the desk, a paper towel to her head, as it caught the blood that was still pouring from the wound on her head. "What on earth have you done?" he asked, as he saw the little pile of paper towels on the desk, all badly stained with her blood. He caught up a couple of new ones, and held them to her head. Head wounds always bled a lot, but she seemed to be bleeding excessively. "I tripped, fell and hit my head on the door frame" she mumbled. "I haven't been able to stop the bleeding." He looked at the wound, and shook his head. "I'm not surprised" he said, "This needs suturing. I'll take you down to the accident department, and we'll get it stitched. You'd better lock up and I'll take you in the car."

"I can't" she said. "Uncle told me to get on with the work, and I won't be able to do that if I have to go to the hospital."

"It's got to be stitched Deborah" he said urgently. "It won't stop bleeding properly otherwise, and it will scar badly." he looked at the area where she had fallen. "What did you trip over to hit the frame with such force?" he asked, but she shook her head, wincing as her headache increased. "Uncle pushed me, and I fell" she said, but Hayden's eyes had already seen the bruise that was beginning on the other side of her face. "He hit you, didn't he?" he said quietly, and she nodded. "I was late coming back from the post office" she said, "and he was waiting for me. I normally duck, if I see him standing there, but today, I didn't, and the

blow pushed me off balance. He's gone out to lunch anyway now."
"So, when is your lunch break?" he asked, but she didn't look at him, as she said, "I don't have a lunch break. I don't eat anything anyway, so he decided it's a good idea for me not to have a break, just work all the way through until 5.00 when I go home."
"So why don't you eat anything?" he asked, and was shocked at her reply. "Aunty doesn't leave any bread out for me to bring into work. She sometimes forgets to put out enough bread for Uncle and myself to have any toast for breakfast, so I have to go without. He wouldn't go without, because he likes his food too much."
"Deborah, are you telling me that you sometimes go through the day without eating anything?" she nodded, and he asked. "Why can't you buy something for yourself from the cafe on your way into work?"
"Because I don't have any money" she said. "Now, can we just forget about it please? Can't you get me a plaster or something to put over this cut?"
"No." he said angrily. "It needs to be stitched, and as you won't let me take you to hospital, then I can see I'll have to do it myself."
"Don't be ridiculous" she said. "You can't stitch it; a plaster would be okay."
"It won't" he said. "Don't you know that I'm a doctor? I'll get my case, stitch that wound, and you'll be okay."
"I didn't know." she said. "Thank you"
"Stay seated, and put some pressure on that wound, and I'll be back in a minute." and he was gone, to return in a very few minutes carrying a doctor's case. He was quick while suturing the wound, and when the

wound was stitched, he wiped her face clear of blood, and put a dressing pad in place. He cleared up after himself, then sat beside her. “Now,” he said quietly. “Tell me everything. My grandmother told me that this was originally your father's company, and Susie in the cafe told me he left everything to you when he died? So why don't you have any money to buy food?”
She nodded, and winced as the movement hurt her head. She knew she wanted to tell somebody and had decided to trust him for she had liked him immediately they had met, he had been kind to her, and she had had no kindness shown to her for a long time. “Yes, Dad died, when I was 17. My aunt and uncle told me to leave things to them, and they would deal with everything for me, and I went to live with them. Things seemed to be okay, the manager was in charge here, and the business was doing well. I took all my exams, passed them, and I had hoped to go to university, and as I thought I was going to get some money from dad's estate, I'd be able to move back into my dad’s house, but then my uncle told me he'd decided it would be easier if he and my aunt moved into Dad’s house, to be nearer the office, and he told me that he was going to take over the company. It was when I asked for some money from the estate, to be able to buy some clothes before I went away, that uncle told me that they had cancelled my place at university, they were going to look after everything for me, and I'd have to work for him in future, and buying clothes was a waste of money. He pays me peanuts for doing this work, makes me cook for him and aunt and do all the housework. She does nothing all day apart from buying some food, but normally she just sits watching

television and eating chocolates." she drew in a deep breath. "Please, I haven't told you all this, if he found out, then he'd be very angry."

"Not half as angry as I am, having heard that." he thought for a minute. "What did the solicitors say?" She laughed mirthlessly at his question. "Absolutely nothing. His solicitor is his son, Dudley. He engineers everything to his father's benefit."

"What about your solicitor?" he frowned, "You must have had one, or your father must have had one?"

"Yes, he did. As soon as the estate was sorted, he got given the sack by my uncle."

"Give me his name, and I'll see what I can do for you." Deborah nodded. "His name was Mr. Rickards, and his offices are just down the road from here. He was kind to me when Dad died, but then Uncle Arthur took over and Dudley told him he wasn't needed any more." Hayden nodded, as he assimilated the information. "Don't fret Deborah, I'm not going to give my work to your uncle after the way I've seen him treat you. There is no way your father would have wanted you to be treated like this. As an outsider I can see that there are things that need to be done, and the first thing is that you need some time to recover after your accident. I'm going to take you home, so you can recover."

"No, you can't" she pleaded. "He'll be so angry, and I wouldn't be able to rest anyway. My aunt would insist that I'd have more time to do the housework." Hayden was shocked, but tried to hide it. "Well, it's his own fault" he said, then smiled as Deborah asked, "How did you know my name anyway? We've never met before."

"My grandmother told me that Mr. Parkes secretary

was called Anne, but his daughter was called Deborah and she showed me an article in the paper and you were with him, and I wondered where she was and why you were doing the work. I didn't know, until Susie from the cafe, told me, about your uncle giving the previous secretary the sack. But don't worry about that now. When you're Uncle comes back, I'll tell him I took you to hospital, because as a medical person, I don't think its correct that you should have to carry on working after such an accident. I'd prefer to take you to hospital and have your head x rayed in case you've got a fracture, and you can be kept in overnight to rest and recover. Now, get your coat on, and I'll take you," and her head aching fit to burst, she did as she had been told.

When her uncle returned, from his lunch, he was almost incandescent with rage that Deborah was not there, until Hayden walked in. "Where's that ungracious niece of mine?" her uncle queried, but Hayden kept his cool. "I just came to let you know that I've taken Deborah to hospital, and she's being kept in overnight" he said. "I came back to see you, and found her bleeding heavily from a bad head wound. It's been stitched, but because she was also concussed, they're keeping her in for observation. Hope that's not going to cause any problems for you" he said, his tone indicating that he didn't care if it would or not. "No, no problem." Her uncle's tone indicated that there would be. "What hospital is she in?" he asked, but Hayden didn't answer. "She'll probably need about four or five days off to recover fully" he said, and watched the older man grow red in the face. "It will be very inconvenient" he said. "But I suppose she'll have to stay in. Was there a reason why you needed to see me again?" he asked, but Hayden shook his head. "No, it's been sorted now. I'll see you again soon. Goodbye" and he left the office. As he walked away, to return to his grandmother's house, he was looking forward to making some waves in the near future.

Chapter Two

Deborah opened her eyes and lay against the pillows the following morning, watching the activity in the ward around her. She had been taken there after being examined in the accident department, it had been busy then, and she couldn't understand why they had kept her in. Her head was still aching, and when she looked in the mirror on the locker, she could see the bruises on her face. The side her uncle had hit, was bruised but where she had hit the door frame was a mass of stitches, dried blood and a very big bruise that stretched into her hair line, and down under her chin. The young nurse who had come to wake her, smiled as she looked at her. “Hello Deborah” she said, “I'm Nurse Evans. Did you sleep well?” she asked. “I've just got to take your temperature and pulse if you don't mind.” Deborah submitted to the ministrations, and watched as the nurse noted the findings on her chart. “Am I going to be okay to go home today?” she asked, but the nurse shook her head. “I don't know” she replied. “That's going to be up to the consultant to decide. His registrar will come and do a round later on this morning, and make a decision. I don't think you will be fit enough. You were quite badly concussed you know. I think he'll want to keep you in and see how you are.” She looked round her at the activity behind her. “Nurse Davis will bring you a cup of tea and your breakfast in a minute, and then we'll get you up and take you to have a wash.”
“Thank you very much” said Deborah, and lay back against the pillows, as she wondered what her uncle

and aunt would say to her when she eventually got home. Mr. Tomlinson had been very good to her yesterday, looking after her head wound, sewing it up for her, and then bringing her here to the hospital, but he wasn't going to be around, and she would have to deal with her relatives herself. At that moment, a nurse bought a tray to her, with her breakfast, and she ate it quickly. "Do you want any more?" the nurse who had taken her temperature enquired, and she nodded. "If it's not a problem, I'd love some" she said, "I haven't eaten much for the last couple of days, and I'm quite hungry." The nurse smiled. "I'll go and get some more bread and butter for you." she said. "There's always some over. Some of the older patients don't eat much at all," She was soon back with another plate of food, and more tea, and gratefully Deborah was able to make a full meal. After breakfast, she was allowed to get up with the aid of the nurse, and tried to walk to the bathroom, where she was to have a wash, but her head was spinning, and the nurse put her back to her bed, and bought her a bowl of water instead. She was glad to lay down again, and slid into sleep. She was woken by the arrival of a man in a white coat, who stood by her bed and took her pulse. "Morning" he said, with a smile. "I'm Jake Lovell, the registrar. I was on duty when you were admitted yesterday, and I've come to see how you are. How do you feel today?"

"I'm okay, when I'm laying down, but I tried to get up and walk to the bathroom, and nearly fell over, so the nurse had to put me back to bed."

"That's what I was worried about" he said. "I think we're going to keep you in for a couple of days, and make sure that the concussion doesn't do any lasting harm." He grinned at her. "If I were you, I'd stay in bed for a while, catch up on your sleep, and just take it easy. Don't read or watch television will you, otherwise it could cause a problem with your eyes." He frowned. "Do you have any relatives who will want to visit?"

"Well, I've got relatives, but I don't think they'll visit. They'll want me to get back to work as soon as possible anyway, so a day in bed sounds like heaven." He grinned at her. "Okay, we'll keep you in bed today. I'll be back to see you tomorrow." and he walked away. Deborah lay back against the pillows, took the tablets given to her for her headache, which was still there, and went back to sleep again. After a good lunch, which she ate eagerly, she was surprised to see Hayden Tomlinson walking up the ward when visiting time arrived, to where she lay, accompanied by another man, who was carrying a briefcase. "Hi Deborah" Hayden said, "This is Mr. Rickards, who was your father's solicitor. How do you feel today?"

"I'm okay, just a bit dizzy when I try to walk and I've still got a headache, so Mr. Lovell told me to stay in bed today, and he'd reconsider tomorrow." She smiled at the other man. "Hello Mr. Rickards. We did meet a few years ago, when you came to see me after Dad died, and then you came to the funeral as well."

"Yes," he agreed, shaking her hand. "But I didn't expect to see you looking like this. What on earth happened to you Deborah? You've lost so much weight since your father died, and I've been told that your aunt and uncle have moved into your father's house, and your uncle has taken over your father's company.

He didn't want you to sell it, but I wasn't able to do anything, because your uncle didn't want me involved after I'd sorted out the estate. He said his own solicitor would deal with everything." Hayden Tomlinson looked at him. "Mr. Rickards," he said softly, "I think it would be a good idea, if we were to go into one of the side rooms, where we can have a private talk with Deborah. We don't want her private affairs shouted over the ward." The older man agreed, and shortly, Deborah was installed into a wheel chair, and with a gown over her nightdress, and a blanket over her knees, she was pushed into a side room, and the two men made themselves comfortable in the hospital chairs. "Now," said Mr. Rickards. "Let's start at the beginning, shall we? Deborah, what happened after your uncle sacked me? Did you sign any paperwork to do with the company?"

Deborah took a deep breath, and began to talk. "I've signed nothing at all. After Dad died, I stayed with my uncle and aunt in their house, and Dad's house was left empty. I would go and make sure it was okay, because I wanted to live in it, and hoped that when I was 18, I'd be able to leave my aunt and uncle and make myself a home in it, and I knew that I'd be able to get access to Dad's money, so I'd be able to afford to live there. I was going to go to university but I'd have a place to return to in the holidays. You'd already told me that I'd have enough money, and I'd been offered a place at Warwick. About a month before my 18th birthday, my uncle and his son Dudley, who is his solicitor and deals with everything for him, came with me to see the house, looked around it, and they were nodding and looked pleased with themselves. When we'd gone back to my Uncle's house, they sat me down, and told me that as Dad's company needed to continue, they were going to get rid of the manager that Dad had installed, and they had decided that my Uncle would take over the job of running it, and as the house was so near it, it would be easier if he and Aunt Claudia moved in to it, so he could walk to work every day. (He doesn't, but that's another story). Anyway, I said I didn't think they should move in, because I was going to live there myself, and Dudley said that as he had power of attorney over my affairs, which incidentally, I don't think he did, it would be easier for his parents to move in. I got cross with them both at that time, but they wouldn't listen. I asked for some money to be able to buy some clothes for when I went to Uni, and it was then they told me they'd cancelled my place at university anyway, so I wasn't able to go to it, and I didn't know what else I could do. So, they moved into the house, and again I asked for some money, but Uncle told me that new clothes were a waste of money and he didn't think it would be a good idea to spend my money on rubbish. I thought there was some money left because Dad always said that I'd be well looked after, but I didn't query too much. Anyway, they moved into the house, I went with them, and I was about to move back into my old bedroom, when Aunt told me that that that room would be saved for guests, and I could have the smaller box room." she sighed, thinking back to her original room. "A day after that, an enormous skip arrived, and they chucked out all my things from when I was a child, and I was only able to save a couple of things that my mother had given me. I objected of course, but they didn't listen to a word I said. They started getting rid of all dad's furniture as well, and bringing in some of their own, only keeping a few items that they liked. A couple of weeks after that, my aunt told me that she couldn't get a housekeeper quickly, and asked, would I be able to do some cooking for her, because I'd done a course in French cookery when I was at school. And it carried on from there, I gradually had to do all the cooking and the housework, and she never did get a housekeeper. I'd done a course of shorthand and typing at school, because I thought I'd be able to give Dad a hand to run the company before I went to Uni, and gradually, Uncle decided that I would be able to do all his office work for him, and its continued. When I asked for a proper salary, he laughed, but then said it was only fair, and they give me a few pounds a month. They said I had to pay for board and lodging with them, and that's why they can't pay me a full salary." Hayden Tomlinson drew in a deep breath at this. "So why didn't you say anything to them?" he asked, but Deborah shook her head. "You can see what he did to me just for being two minutes late back from the post office" she said, pointing to the bruises on her face. "That is nothing compared with what he did when I told him that I wanted my share of the company money, and my house back." She grimaced, "I had two black eyes for over a week after that, bruises everywhere else, my left wrist hurt for ages, and I think it was actually broken, because it didn't work properly for a long time, and it hurt to breathe for a few weeks afterwards. He and Dudley together are a lethal combination. Dudley was holding me, and my uncle was hitting me. They kept me in the house until the bruises had gone down, so nobody saw what they'd done to me. It's been easier and a lot less painful to say nothing and accept everything. You probably think I'm a coward, but I'm not, honestly. Mr. Rickards, I've never signed anything, so I would think that they are just doing everything to suit themselves. They were always jealous of Dad and his success, and Mum, before she died, always told me that her sister and her husband would do anything to get as much money as they could. They like money, as you can see from my uncle's car and his clothes." She sighed and leant back in the chair, and watched as the solicitor produced some papers from his briefcase. "The will your father made after your mother died, left everything to you, apart from a bequest to a charity, which was paid when the will was settled. Your uncle was the executor of the will, but he didn't have the right to take everything from you. As far as I'm concerned, you should have control of your father's company, and you should also have the house, along with a substantial amount of money, which was left. You say you've signed nothing at all?" he asked, and she nodded. "I've never been asked to sign anything." she said quietly. "I've had to work as a secretary to my uncle, be a cook/housekeeper to him and his wife since they moved into the house, and that was over three years ago. I had my 21st birthday last April, and Dad died when I was 17, three months before my 18th birthday."

The solicitor nodded. "Your cousin doesn't have power of attorney over your affairs "he said. "I had that until you were 21, and I was very worried when I was told that my services were no longer required. I will need all details of your cousin's address and his full name" he continued, "I think I'm going to do a bit of checking up for you. But in the meantime, would you be willing for me to act for you?" Deborah nodded. "I would, please Mr. Rickards. I'm old enough now to be able to look after my own affairs, and if anybody queried anything, I could say that I'd decided I needed my own legal advisor." The solicitor grinned at her, and she knew he would do all he could for her, then he frowned as he looked closely at her. "You must not go back to the house alone, Deborah" he said, now grim faced, "to do so would allow them to take over control of your life again."

"But I've got to go back." she cried. "I don't have any of my clothes, and everything I own is back there. I've got to go back to get them. And where else am I meant to go? I don't have any other relatives, and I haven't got any money to be able to go to a hotel."

"You're coming back with me" Hayden Tomlinson said quietly. "I'm going to take you to stay with my grandmother. She met your father when he did some work for her a few years ago, and they were good friends before that. That's why I was seeing your uncle about getting some more work done for her. She wasn't aware that your father had passed away, until I told her, but she's very angry about how they're treating you, and she will agree with us, you're not going to go back to the house while that man is still in residence."

"I don't know your grandmother" she argued, but he was adamant. "I've told her what happened yesterday, and when you're discharged from here, she has invited you to go and stay with her. Mr. Rickards and I will accompany you, and we will take you to the house to collect your belongings. That way, neither your aunt or uncle will be able to stop you. You will have your solicitor and your doctor in attendance with you." He grinned at the solicitor. "I think you are looking forward to making sure that Deborah gets her rightful inheritance, aren't you?" The solicitor nodded and smiled at her. "Don't fret my dear. We'll make sure that things are going to improve from now on."

Laying back against the pillows that night, as she settled for sleep, Deborah thought back to the events of that afternoon, and grinned to herself. Her two visitors had left her alone after their discussion, and she had been bemused by the speed of their actions while they were with her. They had made a plan of action, and she had agreed to move into stay with Hayden's grandmother after she had been discharged. Hayden had talked to the registrar, when he visited her that afternoon, who seemed to be a little in awe at her visitor, and she wondered why, but hadn't asked anything. He had said she would be fit to be discharged within a couple of days, dependent on her recovery, and the two men had said their goodbyes and left her alone. The Sister of the ward had been very nice to her, ensuring she had enough to eat, and she wondered why everybody was being so polite to her, but decided it was just because of her injury, and they wanted to make sure that she was recovering well. She closed her eyes and slept soundly all night long.

The following afternoon, she had been laying on top of the bed, thinking about things, and had been

pleased to see Hayden come and visit her again. She had been allowed to take another short walk, and her head hadn't reacted badly at all, so she was going to be discharged the following day. He had sat with her, talking about nothing in particular, and had gone to talk to the ward Sister, regarding her discharge. She had laid back against the pillows, when her uncle had stalked into the ward, and disregarding everybody else, he had marched up to her bed. He grabbed her wrist, and pulled her upright. "Come on, you're leaving. Laying around, making the most of a cut. You're leaving now. Get dressed". He had pulled the curtains around her bed, after he had found her clothes in the locker, and thrown them on the bed. He had hold of her wrist, and pulled her to the edge of the bed. "I can't leave, Uncle" she said loudly. "The doctors have told me I've got to stay in."
"There's nothing wrong with you" he growled, pulling her upright. "Get dressed now." He raised his hand, and hit her face hard. She gasped, and put a hand to her face, but he grabbed it, and pulled her nearly off of the bed. "You'll get more of that if you don't do what you're told to do" he said, and he left her to get dressed, while he stood outside and waited.

In the office Hayden was talking to the ward sister, when they noticed the activity and saw the curtains being pulled around the bed. Hayden was on his feet, and about to leave the office, when he saw Mr. Cummins leave the cubicle and wait impatiently outside. "Call Security please Sister" he said, "tell them to come urgently" and he waited while she did that. "Now let's go and see what's happening" he said, and they walked swiftly to where the older man waited. "What are you doing" Sister asked. She glanced inside the cubicle, where Deborah was standing by the side of the bed. "Miss Parkes, please get back onto the bed again. I don't know why you are trying to get dressed, but you can't leave until the consultant has told you that you are fit enough."

"Stop interfering woman. My niece is coming home with me now. She's putting it on. She's just got a cut on her head. Taking up a bed when it's not necessary." blustered the older man. He didn't see Hayden, his attention taken up with trying to get Deborah out of the ward. The other patients and visitors on the ward had been disturbed by the activity, and now everybody was trying to see what was happening. "She is not leaving," said Sister. "She has had a very nasty concussion, and needs to rest and recover. I'm afraid I must ask you to leave. I shall call Security otherwise."

"Oh, shut up woman, and don't interfere." he hissed at her, and called loudly, "Get dressed Deborah. Your aunt needs you."

"I don't think so Mr. Cummins." Hayden said loudly from behind him, and he turned to see the tall man. "Deborah has been admitted for rest and recovery following a very nasty concussion, which was caused when you hit her." There were gasps from some of the other patients in adjacent beds.

"I did nothing of the sort," the older man blustered, but Hayden continued, "You hit her, and she fell and injured herself. She now has a concussion, and needs to recover from that. She will not be leaving with you, today, or at any other time. And now, I think it's time you left the hospital."

"What's it got to do with you?" her uncle sneered, and Hayden said very quietly. "Deborah and I are to be married" he said quietly. "She will stay with one of my relatives before the wedding day, and afterwards she will be with me, obviously."
"She needs my permission before she can get married" her uncle said loudly, but Hayden laughed. "She's over 21. She doesn't need anybody's permission, and in any case, you have never had the right to give that permission." he said. There was a clatter of feet, as the Security team arrived on the ward, and the Sister gave them a brief outline of the story. They escorted Mr. Cummins from the ward, and Hayden watched them go. Sister went behind the curtains, and with help from Hayden, they got Deborah back on the bed. She was white and shaking, and the mark where he had slapped her, stood out in relief. "I don't want to go with him" she muttered, her eyes filling with tears. "Don't make me go, please." Sister sat on the side of the bed and held her hand. "Nobody's going to make you go with him" she said. "And as your fiancée is here, he'll be able to look after you."
"He's not my fiancée" Deborah said. "He doesn't know me. How can he be my fiancée?"
"I had to say something Debby" Hayden said, as he took her hand in his. "I had to get rid of him, and that was the only thing I could think of to tell him. Now, try and get some sleep if you can, and we'll get you moved into a secure room, so he can't sneak in to see you again. I'm sure that would be possible wouldn't it Sister?" he asked the other woman, who nodded. "We'll get you something to make you sleep" he thought for a while, and the Sister said hurriedly, "I'll

call Jake Lovell and get him to write something up for her. I think we'll leave the curtains shut for a while, so the other patients don't ask questions", and she escorted Hayden from the cubicle, and left Deborah alone with her thoughts. She was lying back against the pillows, worrying about what was going to happen, when Jake Lovell came into the cubicle, and took her pulse. "I think we'll give you a little injection" he said. "You'll sleep after that, and we'll move you into a different room, and hopefully you'll feel better in the morning." He picked up her chart, wrote on it, and took it with him, as he left. "Sleep well Deborah" he said, as he left. Minutes later, the Sister appeared and gave her an injection in her arm. It took effect almost immediately, and she was asleep within minutes.

She didn't awake until late in the evening, and opened her eyes to a different view of things. She was in a room on her own, the door was shut, but Hayden was sitting in the armchair watching her, and he smiled as she opened her eyes and looked at him. "Had a good sleep?" he asked and she nodded. "Do you feel any better?" he asked, and she took a good look at him. He was wearing different clothing to that he had been wearing when he had visited earlier, instead of jeans and a sweater, he was wearing a suit, with a sober tie, and looked like a successful business man. "Yes," she said. "I do feel a bit better. My face hurts though" and she raised a hand to her cheek. "He's got a nasty left hand" he said, and suddenly everything that had happened that afternoon came back to her. "He won't be able to find me, will he?" she begged. "Please don't let him find me again." Hayden stood and walked towards her. He reached down and took her hand away from her face, and held it. "He won't be able to find you again. When you're better, I'll take you to stay with my grandmother, and she'll look after you. I promise nobody will be able to take you away, unless you want to go." She sat up, and he pushed her back against the pillows. "Don't fret Debby, just rest, and get better."

"Mum and Dad called me Debby" she said quietly, looking back into the past. "Nobody's called me that since Dad died. Mr. Tomlinson, why on earth did you tell him we were going to get married? Don't be so silly. We've only just met, we don't love each other, and as far as I'm concerned, that's the only reason to get married. What did you have to tell him that for."

"Because I think it's the only way, we are going to get you to break away from him. Do you have anybody else who wants to marry you?"

"Don't be silly" she said again, "I don't meet anybody. I haven't been allowed to go out with anybody since Dad died, and I went to live with my aunt and uncle."

"Right then, if your uncle and aunt think that we are going to be married, they won't be able to get you to go back to them to be their unpaid housekeeper, cook and secretary. They will believe that you and I will be living together, I can care for you, and you will be under my protection. If you think about it Debby, if you are single, living alone and earning a living, there would always be the risk that they would come and find you, take you back to the house, and keep you there, looking after them, and making you, their slave. This way, if you and I are married, you'd have my name, my protection, and they'd have no legal claim on you at all.

You're over 21 anyway, so they can't force you, and they might try that, if you're still single. I don't intend we would be married in the fullest sense of the word, we could share a house, but not a bed, and if you find somebody in the future, who you could be happy with, and want to marry, then the marriage could be annulled without too many problems." he squeezed her hand. "What do you say Debby, will you marry me?"

"May I think about it?" she said, and he nodded. "Not for too long though. We'll have to make a decision soon." She smiled at him, and yawned. "You're tired" he said. "I'll leave you to get some sleep, and I'll be back in the morning. Sleep well Debby" and he bent his head and kissed her on the cheek. She watched as the door shut behind him, and yawned again. Then she turned on her side, and was asleep in minutes.

She woke from a deep sleep, to hear an altercation in the corridor, and lay awake listening to the noise. She could hear heavy feet tramping outside the door, and then, heard her uncle's voice. "Where is she?" he was bellowing. "She was here this afternoon. Where have you put her?" She could hear doors being opened and closed, and knew he was looking for her, so she slipped out of bed, and ran into the en suite bathroom, and shut the door. She heard the door into her room open, and looked fearfully at the door of the bathroom, which she had locked behind her. She could hear other voices now, including two women, telling everybody to be quiet, so the patients could sleep, then a deep voice – Hayden's. "Mr. Cummins. Your niece has been taken to stay with my relative. She is no longer in the hospital. You must leave now. Security are here, and have called the police. I'm sure that charges will now be bought against you." She could hear her uncle shouting, "you can't do this, take your hands off me." then a scuffle, before there was a loud thud, then silence. The hum of voices died down a bit, and she stood silently, wanting to know what was happening, but unwilling to open the door. There was a soft knock at the door, but she wouldn't open it, then a louder knock at the bathroom door. "Debby" she could hear Hayden's voice. "Debby, it's all right. He's gone. Come out." Reluctantly she slid back the bolt, and opened the door a crack. Hayden was standing outside the door, and as she opened it, he looked at her and smiled. "Well, that was interesting, wasn't it?" He held out his hand, and took hers. "Come on Debby. He's gone, and he won't be allowed back in. But I think you'd be better off, if I take you to my grandmother's house now."

"At this time of night?" she said, for she could see from the windows that it was night time. He smiled, as he led her back into the room. "It's only 10.00 at night. The night staff are on duty, but they were all told that he might try something again, which is why there were a couple of extra people around. But I can understand why you don't want to go this late. First thing in the morning, I'll take you to her house, and you can stay there and recover." He hesitated, then, "get back into bed, and I'll get somebody to bring you a drink, and you can calm down a bit, and have something to eat, because I don't think you've had any supper, then tomorrow morning, we'll go and see my grandmother. Does that sound okay?" She nodded, and he smiled at her again, pulled the bedclothes back, and helped her back into the bed. She could feel him taking her pulse, and now, he produced a torch from his pocket, and told her to stare straight at him, before he tested her pupil reaction. "Have you got a headache?" he asked, and she nodded. "It's not too bad" she said, "but it's there, and I hope it doesn't get any worse"

"It won't" he said "we'll give you something for it." he turned away from the bed. "I'll go and sort out a drink and something to eat for you." and he left the room.

The nurse she had seen the night before, came in with a tray, on which she found some sandwiches and a pot of tea. "Mr. Tomlinson, said you're to have these after you've eaten the sandwiches" she said, holding out a small medicine cup in which were two tablets, "and have a drink, then settle down to sleep again." She looked at Deborah, with an expression she couldn't understand, "I'll come back for the tray in a short while." and she left the room. Left alone, Deborah ate the sandwiches, drank all the tea, took her tablets and lay back against the pillows, wondering why Hayden was being so nice to her. If it was pity, he felt, then she didn't want it. But he had arranged for Mr. Rickards to help her, and he was trying to stop her uncle being able to take over her life again. Sleepily, she thought of his strange proposal, and knew if he made it again, she would accept. She closed her eyes, and drifted into sleep.

Chapter Three

Two weeks later, Deborah stood with Hayden, in front of the registrar, who had inspected the licence which Hayden had produced, and performed their wedding. The two weeks had been busy, and had also solved a few problems that she had had. Accompanied by Hayden and Mr. Rickards, she had been taken back to her own house, at a time when her uncle was not there, and she had been able to locate all her personal items, and the two items of her mother's she had saved when her uncle had thrown everything else out – her work box and a small music box. She had taken all the photo albums she could find, but when she tried to locate her mother's jewellery, which she knew had been left in the house, she was unable to do so. Her aunt had stayed in the sitting room, but when they were about to leave, she had come into the hallway. "You'll regret taking up with him" she had said. "You had a good home here, and you wouldn't have had to worry about the future. On your own head be it." and she had turned to walk away. "I had a good home?" Deborah queried loudly, then laughed, mirthlessly, "on the contrary Aunt Claudia, you had a good home. You and your despicable husband stole my father's company, moved into my family home and threw all my possessions away, didn't allow me much food, made me act as unpaid cook, housekeeper and secretary, and you think I had a good home?" her voice rose, but her aunt said nothing further. Hayden had gone after her aunt, taken her arm, and quietly said a few things to her, and the woman had gone white, before going back into the sitting room, and closing the door. When Deborah had asked him what he had said, he refused to say, and she had been driven away from the house, with regret, for she and her parents had been happy there, and she didn't think she'd ever be able to go back to live there. And so, today was her wedding day. There were no guests, apart from his grandmother, and her companion, who were to act as witnesses. Deborah was wearing a suit which she had bought for the occasion, in light blue wool, with a white silk blouse. She wasn't wearing anything on her head, and her blonde hair hung down her back, in a cloud. Hayden had bought a selection of wedding rings to his grandmother's house, one evening, when he had visited, and she had chosen the plainest and simplest of them all. The registrar had asked them each a few questions, then the service started, and soon, Hayden was putting the ring onto her finger. She didn't feel in the least married, as he took her by the hand and led her outside to the corridor. “Right,” he said shortly. “we'll all go back to grandmother's house, and have lunch, and then we'll have a talk. Grandmother” he raised his voice slightly, for the old lady was a trifle deaf, “thank you and Estelle for being our witnesses. I'll drive Deborah back to your house now, and we'll see you there.” He watched as Estelle, the companion, escorted the old lady to the lift, and the doors shut behind them, then led her to the stairs, and they walked downstairs. His car was drawn up outside, and he opened the door for her, and then shut it, once she was installed on the front seat. “Put your seat belt on” he instructed, as he came to sit beside her, and she did as she had been told. The drive back to the house was accomplished in silence, Deborah didn't feel like talking, and Hayden had been quiet since he collected her that morning. As the gates of the house closed behind the car, she looked in renewed surprise at the old lady's house. She couldn't believe that she was able to stay there, when Hayden had taken there, on her release from hospital. She had often seen it before, when she had been walking around the town when her parents were alive, but hadn't realised who lived in it. It was a large house, flat fronted, with a central front door, with three large windows on either side, and seven windows on the first floor. There were more windows above that, on the second floor, smaller than the ones below, and the roof rose steeply from that

As Hayden escorted her from the car, and up the stairs to the front door, she recalled her first arrival, when Hayden had bought her home from the hospital. The registrar - Jake - had visited early in the morning, and told her that she could go, and she had been dressed and ready to leave when Hayden entered the room. "Okay?" he asked, and she nodded. "I've seen Sister and she said you're okay to leave, so I think we'll get you to my grandmother's house as soon as we can. That way, if your uncle does come back, which I don't think he will be able to do, then she'll be able to tell him, with all truth, that you're not here. However, after he was arrested last night, I don't think he'll want to come back any time soon. He was taken to the police station late last night."
"He was arrested?" she questioned, and he nodded, and grinned at the remembrance. "He turned up last

night when he tried to find you, but wasn't able to, and when the security team and the police turned up, he managed to hit one of them, and he was arrested and dragged off in handcuffs. The police were going to keep him in until late this morning, so we can drive away from here in safety." She shuddered, and he took her hand in his. "He's not going to be able to hurt you again." he said. "The police have asked if you would be able to give a statement about his behaviour towards you, about the way he's hit you in the past, and this week, and they will keep that on record in case you want to charge him with assault, which I think you should do. They've already taken note of your injuries when you were admitted and taken photos, and Jake took photos after your uncle had slapped you when you were in the ward, and of course the hospital photographed your bruises when you were brought in. So, if you're ready, we'll go." She had said her thanks to the ward sister and the staff who had looked after her, and accompanied by Hayden, had left the hospital. When he had stopped the car outside the front door, she had looked in astonishment at the house, and when a butler had opened the door, her jaw had dropped. "Close your mouth Debby, you look like a stranded fish" he muttered, and led her towards a set of double doors, which he opened and ushered her inside. If she had been surprised at the house, she had been even more astonished at his grandmother. The old lady was tall, stoutly built, and walked with a stick. She had snow white hair, pulled back into a bun, which made her face appear very angular, and Debby's heart had sunk into her boots when she first saw her. The old lady had been sitting by the fire, and the two woman, one so old, and one so young, summed each other up. Deborah had felt a trifle disconcerted for this was no cosy grandmother who would give grandchildren a hug, but a woman who was obviously the matriarch of the entire family. But she was escorted forwards, and the old lady had put out a hand to shake hers. "This is Deborah Parkes, grandmother" Hayden said, and the old lady smiled at her. "Deborah, it's so lovely to see you again" she said, and her face had changed, and she had looked welcoming, and suddenly Deborah felt as if she had come home.

"Again?" questioned Deborah, for she wasn't aware that she'd ever met the woman before. "Yes, but I know you won't have remembered our first meeting. Your grandmother and I were very good friends from when we were at school together, and your father and mother bought you with her, when she came to see me, when you were about three weeks old. Soon after that, your grandmother passed away, and your parents and I lost contact until I needed some work done on this house, and remembered he owned a building firm. We became very good friends, and I was so sorry to hear that your mother had passed away when you were younger. He had done some more work for me shortly before he died, but I was unaware that he had passed away. That's why I asked Hayden to get some estimates from your company, but when I found out how your uncle treated you, and how he'd taken over the company, then we made a decision not to give him any work." Hayden had been watching Deborah's face. "I think you've shocked Debby" he said. "Maybe we should ask Mrs Watts to take her to her room, and she can freshen up, before we all have coffee." His grandmother agreed, and the housekeeper, when summoned, escorted Deborah up to the room she was to stay in.

She had enjoyed staying with the old lady – she had many stories to tell her of her grandmother, a woman she could not remember at all, and she learned a lot about her family from her. Hayden had told her he didn't want her going out shopping without him, but he had several things he had to get on with and was unable to take her out, so because she desperately needed some new clothes, he had phoned one of the large shops nearby, and an assistant had come to the house, complete with boxes and boxes of clothes, which Deborah was allowed to make a choice from. "I can't afford to buy clothes" she had said to Hayden, when he told her of his arrangements, but he had smiled. "You will be able to, once Mr. Rickards gets his teeth into the problem. You can pay me back then, if you really need to." he had replied, and reassured, Deborah had chosen the clothes she had wanted to be able to wear for years, but had not been able to. Hayden had told her to buy something to wear for the wedding, and although she had once dreamed of wearing white satin and lace, she knew it was not for her, and instead had chosen the blue suit.

That morning, after the housekeeper had given her breakfast in bed, she had bathed and dressed herself, and made sure her hair and face were suitable for a wedding day. Most of the bruises had gone, although the scar was still visible on the side of her face, but she had pulled her hair forwards, and it almost hid the defect. She had gone downstairs and found everybody waiting for her. Lady Grimes had smiled as she looked at her, and said "Very nice my dear. That colour suits you very well," but Hayden hadn't said anything nice to her at all, just asked if she had her birth certificate, before escorting her out to his car, and driven them both to the registry office.

When Hayden accompanied her into the sitting room, after the ceremony, she was surprised to see that there were quite a few vases of flowers scattered around the room, and their aroma filled the air. "Oh, they're lovely" she said, and Hayden smiled at her. "Well, you didn't have a bouquet, so I thought I'd make sure you had something nice when you got here. I'm sorry, but there won't be a wedding cake, but I know Mrs. Watts is cooking a really good meal for you."

"Well, we're not exactly celebrating, are we?" she asked with a smile, and was surprised to see an odd expression on his face. "No, we're not" he answered her, "but it is your wedding day, and as such it should be special." He went and sat down in the chair by the fireplace. "Tomorrow, you can move into my house, and we can have a chat with Mr. Rickards. I know he's found out a few things, and he'll tell you exactly what they are." She had taken a seat away from him, looking out onto the garden, as the door opened, and his grandmother entered. She looked at them both and shook her head. "You could at least make a pretence of being a happily married couple" she said. "Honestly, it looks as though you can't stand the sight of each other, and you've only been married an hour or so."

"Well, we didn't exactly marry for love" Hayden

argued. "I hope we can be friends, but it's not as if we can't keep our hands off each other, like Ella did, when she got married. That reception was embarrassing, I can tell you."

"Who's Ella?" Deborah asked, and Hayden grinned. "One of my cousins. She married about a year ago, and she and her new husband couldn't keep their hands off each other. I'm surprised they managed to last as long as they did, before they left for their honeymoon."

"Hayden!" his grandmother said. "That will be enough of that. It was nice to see that she was so in love with him. I'm glad that they still feel like that about each other."

"Oh, it's nice" he agreed, "but like I said, I and a few others felt as if we were intruding." His grandmother laughed, and nodded. "She's happy at least. It's a pity that you two won't be as happy."

"Oh, we'll be fine" Hayden said. "A perfect marriage – no emotions involved, and the freedom to do what we want, when we want. And then, if Debby does fall head over heels with somebody, and wants to marry him, we'll have a quick annulment, and nobody will be unhappy." Deborah sat in her chair, wondering what she had done. The way Hayden was talking, was making her feel very unhappy, and she didn't know why. She stood up, and walked to the door "I'll just go upstairs" she said, and almost ran from the room. Somehow, she didn't want to stay with her husband and his grandmother, especially not wearing the suit she had chosen especially for her wedding. It seemed to her, that Hayden was regretting having asked her to marry him. She sighed as she got changed, into a different skirt and a jumper. She didn't want to continue to wear the suit, because it felt as if she were wearing a fancy dress costume. When she had changed, she knew that she had to go downstairs again, even though she wanted to be alone for a while. She had become accustomed to being on her own, with only her thoughts for company, and to be with other people made her feel uncomfortable. She had spent a lot of the past two weeks with Hayden's grandmother, and although she got on well with the older lady, there had been times when she just wanted to be on her own, and had spent quite a bit of time in the library of the house, ostensibly reading, but in reality, thinking about her future. There was a knock at the door, and she sighed, and went to open it. Estelle, Hayden's grandmother's companion was standing there, smiling at her. "Lady Grimes sent me to see if you were okay. You did leave the room fairly quickly, and she hoped that you were feeling alright."

"Thanks Estelle, I'm fine, honestly, I am. I just wanted to be on my own, if you know what I mean." she sighed, then, "I don't mean to be unsociable, it's just that I've been on my own for a long time, and I'm not used to being with people."

"Do you want me to go away?" Estelle asked, but Deborah shook her head. "Does it sound odd, if I say I don't want to be alone with Hayden and his grandmother?" she asked, and Estelle shook her head. "I can't imagine how you must be feeling. You're married to a man who you don't love, and who doesn't love you, and you've only married him to be safe from your uncle and aunt. Don't fret Deborah, I'm sure that everything will work itself out, and you'll be happy with your new life. I'll tell Lady Grimes that you want to be alone for a while, but you'll be down for dinner, if that's what you would like?" Deborah nodded. "Yes please" she said quietly. "I'd actually like to go out for a walk, but Hayden doesn't want me to go out on my own."

"Why not go out into the garden then?" Estelle suggested. "It's big enough that you can walk and get away from people, but you'll be safe."

"That's a good idea." Deborah said. "I think I might just do that. Nobody would object, would they?"

"No, I'm sure that it would be okay. I'll tell Lady Grimes that's what you wanted to do."

"Thanks Estelle" and Deborah watched as the other woman left the room and went downstairs.

Hayden and his grandmother looked through the windows of the room, at Deborah, as she walked slowly round the garden, then Lady Grimes looked at her grandson. "She's not happy, is she?" she said, "I know why she's not, but I had hoped that the wedding would have cheered her up a bit."

"I think she's just realised that she's gone from one form of imprisonment, to another" he answered, and his grandmother shot him a quick glance. "You don't intend to imprison her, do you?" she asked, and he shook his head. "Not in the least. I'll do my level best to try and help her get everything she is owed, returned to her, and let her live her own life. I'd like her to be happy if she can be, and if Rickards can help her, then she'll regain control of her money and hopefully she'll be happier than she is at the moment."

"So, what are you intending to do tomorrow?"

"Nothing, I'll take her to my house, show her round, and when Rickards comes, he might be able to give her

some good news."
"When are you due to start work then?" she asked, and he grinned. "Well, my contract starts in two weeks' time, but I've spent quite a bit of time there already, so I've got a bit of a head start on the job."
"Be nice to Deborah then, for goodness' sake. The poor girl has had so many upsets in her life. Losing her parents, and then having her father's business and the house taken from her, can't be doing her any good. She might have recovered physically from the beating her uncle gave her, but whether her mental state is correct or not, I don't know. This marriage has taken place very quickly, and it must have unsettled her quite a bit." Hayden shot a glance at his grandmother. "Don't you approve of us getting married then?" he asked, and she shook her head. "I don't know. It's the obvious way of preventing her uncle being able to hurt her again, but whether it's the best way for Deborah, I just don't know." she sighed, "Oh Hayden, just be kind to her. Her father told me so much about her when we would talk when he was doing the work on the house. He adored her, wanted her to be happy, and I'd like to think we could make her feel that way."
"I'll try." he said. "I'll take her out for a meal after Rickards has been tomorrow morning, if that would help. We can have a talk when we've had something to eat. If you think that would be a good idea?" he asked with a touch of sarcasm, and his grandmother gave him a sideways look. "Don't be sarcastic Hayden." she said. "But, yes, it is a good idea. Will you be going to visit your parents while you've got time off?" she asked, and he nodded. "Yes, I thought I'd take Deborah up and introduce her to the rest of the family, next week

I've already arranged to go up and collect my new car, so we can do that at the same time."
"Oh, you men and your cars." she said, but turned back to sit by the fireside and Hayden went with her and the subject was changed.

Dinner that night was eaten in the company of Hayden, his grandmother and Estelle, and Deborah found it easy to concentrate on her meal. The housekeeper had provided a superb meal for them, a salmon mousse to start, followed by Noisettes of Lamb, with garden vegetables, and a light as air Castle Pudding to follow. Deborah ate eagerly, for she knew she was too thin. When the saleslady had been with her as she tried on clothes, the other woman had gasped at her thinness. "Oh, my dear" she had said. "You need some more flesh on your bones." than apologised, as she realised what she had said. Deborah had smiled at her, and nodded. "I know I'm too thin" she said. "My diet has been somewhat restricted lately, but I'm sure I'll put it back on soon." And she knew she was putting some pounds back on, and hoped it wasn't going to be too much. When the meal was finished, and they were sitting over coffee in the lounge, Hayden looked at her. "Debby, would you be able to pack tonight, and we can go to my house in the morning? Mr. Rickards will be coming to see us both about 11.00 so I'd like us to be there in plenty of time." She nodded, and wondered exactly where his house was. He'd never told her, and she didn't want to ask in front of his grandmother. "I'll be ready" she said quietly, and put her coffee cup down. "Would anybody object if I went to bed?" she asked, and when nobody said anything to prevent her, she said her good nights and stood to go upstairs. Hayden reached the door before her, and opened it, going with her into the hallway. "Don't worry Debby. Everything's going to be alright. You're safe now from your uncle and aunt. We'll sort something out for you." he bent his head and kissed her gently on the cheek, "Goodnight Debby" he said softly, and watched as she made her way upstairs.

Hayden's house was a surprise to her. It wasn't as large as his grandmother's but it was still bigger than most houses. It had a large garden around it, and she hoped that she would be happy in it, for the time that she would have to live there. The only downside to it, was the fact that it was situated within walking distance of her own house. A large park separated them, but she could easily walk through the park to it. They were greeted by a housekeeper who welcomed her, and produced a tray of coffee for them. "Shall I take Mrs. Tomlinson upstairs and show her the room I've prepared for her?" she asked, but Hayden shook his head. "Not yet Mrs. Bates. I'll do it when we've had a drink." The other woman nodded, and went back to the kitchen, and Hayden escorted her into the sitting room. It was a large apartment, the whole length of the house, with two floor length windows, which looked out onto the drive at the front of the house, but also had a view of the garden, reached by French windows, at the back. It was decorated very nicely – the curtains were burgundy coloured, and the Persian carpet was a lighter shade, and there were several large settees and easy chairs around, along with side tables which small lights on them. She looked

around as she entered, and nodded. “It's lovely” she said quietly, “who decorated it?” He smiled at her, “Thanks, I did. I've always liked trying out colour schemes, and I had a decorator come and do it, but I chose all the colours and the furniture. I did most of the rest of the house as well, apart from some of the bedrooms, which my mother helped me with, and the kitchen, which Mrs. Bates had the last say on. She's been with me since I had my first flat, after I'd qualified, and is what is known in the trade as a 'treasure'.”
“Would she object if I wanted to do anything in the house?” she asked, and he shook his head. “I don't think so. She has help from a couple of daily people, but if you wanted to help, I'm sure she'd welcome the assistance. You can always ask her” He led her to a seat by the fireplace, “Have some coffee, and I'll show you your room, before Mr. Rickards arrives.” She poured the coffee into delicate porcelain cups, and handed one to him, before pouring one for herself. “Now, we've got to have a chat when Mr. Rickards has been” he said. “Talk about money and finances. I think that might depend on what Mr. Rickards has to say, but believe me Debby, you don't have to worry about anything like that. I do have another income apart from what I earn, so you won't bankrupt me. Now, I think we might go and see my parents next week. I won't be able to get up to see them once I've started work at the hospital, because there's going to be a lot of work waiting for me, I can see. They live in Scotland, so we can fly up, but I've found a newer car, which is actually quite near their place, so we'll be able to drive back down. I've got a few things to talk about

with my parents anyway, but they'll be delighted to welcome you as a new daughter."
"Will you tell them the reason for our marriage?" she asked, and he nodded. "I think it would be better for them to know, as we got married so precipitously. Don't worry, they won't say anything to anybody." he grinned at her, and indicated she should drink up. "When you've finished your drink, I'll show you your room." he said, and she did as she had been told.

Her new bedroom was spectacular. It was very large, and looked out over the garden. It had a wall full of wardrobes, and a door led to an en suite bathroom. The curtains were the same light pink colour as the carpet, and matched it perfectly. The bed was a king size, made up with white linen sheets, coloured blankets and covered with a large pink satin bedspread, and the light pink carpet had white fleecy rugs on top of it. There was a day bed near the window, and plenty of room for the bedside table and a small table which could be used as a desk, with chairs to match, and a dressing table with a large mirror on it. "It's lovely" she said. "It's much larger than my original one at my home. Where's your room?" she asked, then blushed, but he didn't say anything, just indicated a door at the other end of the corridor to hers. "Quite close" he said, "I'll be within earshot if you need me at any time." He showed her around the rest of the floor – more bedrooms, each with their own bathroom, as well as storage cupboards and another stair leading to the top floor. "Up there, Mrs. Bates has taken over what were the attics, and they've been made into a bedroom and sitting room. She's got her own kitchen and bathroom up there, and she loves having such a big area for herself. Of course, the house is too large at the moment, but if I ever have children, then it will probably seem smaller." She had gone quite pale at his words, for he had almost indicated that he would like to have children, but not with her, and she felt sad at these words. She didn't say anything, and was almost relieved when she heard the front door bell ring. "That'll be Mr. Rickards," he said, and led the way down to the hallway. The solicitor greeted them both with a large smile. "I hear congratulations are in order" he remarked, as Hayden led the way into the lounge, and indicated a seat. "Thank you." said Hayden, and Deborah nodded. She didn't know what else to say. Hayden offered coffee, but the solicitor refused. "I had a cup just before I left the office" he said. "I'm not going to keep you long, but I wanted to let you know what I had found out when I had discussion recently with your uncle and his solicitor." He withdrew a number of papers from his briefcase and put them on the table, and Hayden led Deborah to it, and they sat together. "Now, this paper is a photocopy of a piece, given to me, by his solicitor, who I understand is your cousin? It supposedly gives complete control of your father's company to your uncle, and is meant to have been signed by you." and he handed her the paper. She looked at it, and shook her head. "That's not my signature" she said. "My writing is completely different to that." The solicitor nodded his head. "That was my impression as well" he said dryly, "and this paper," and he handed her another piece, "supposedly passes control of all monies left by your father, to him as well. And finally, this one, passes the deeds of the house to your uncle." She looked at them all, and shook her head. "This is rubbish." she said angrily. "I've never signed anything, never even seen these papers before, and goes to prove that my uncle and his son, have taken everything my father left for themselves. They even stole my mother's jewellery. That was in the house, but I couldn't find it, and I think my aunt has decided that she wanted it."

"Can you describe it?" Hayden asked, and she nodded. "I can do better than that. One of the photos in the albums is the photo the insurance company took when Dad insured the jewellery. I've got very good pictures of it."

"This has got to be investigated by the police," said the solicitor. "Deborah, may I have a sample of your signature please so that it can be compared, and we can start proceedings against your uncle and aunt, and may I have a copy of the jewellery photo as well. Incidentally, do you know where your cousin is living?" Deborah nodded. "He's taken over the house that my uncle and aunt lived in. They signed it over to him apparently, when they took over my father's house." The solicitor nodded, and put the papers back into the briefcase. "I thought that might be the case" he said, and grinned at them both. Deborah gave him several samples of her signature, and showed him her passport, which had her signature on it, and he grinned. "Got him" he said with ferocious grin. "Right my dears, I'll be in touch with you soon, and we'll see what we can achieve. In the meantime, did you give a statement to the police about the incident that caused your admission to hospital, and sign it?" Deborah nodded, "They took photos of my injuries as well, and of course, the hospital had already taken photos, and they've got those as well" she said, and then smiled as Hayden told the solicitor about her uncle's arrest after he had gone to the hospital to try and force her back to live with them again. "I had heard about it" the solicitor said, "but obviously you don't know the actual truth of the matter until you hear from somebody who was actually on the scene as it were." he turned to Deborah. "I do hope you are going to press charges if you are asked." he said, and she hesitated. "Yes, she will" Hayden spoke. "As my wife, I think it's important that she should get that man off the streets."

"But he's never hit anybody else that I know of," she said, but Hayden took her hand. "No but now he's lost you that he can vent his temper onto, I think he might try and find somebody else who's weaker than he is. He needs teaching a lesson, once and for all." The solicitor nodded, shook their hands, said his farewells, and was gone.

Chapter Four

As the plane took off from Heathrow Airport, Deborah thought back to the events of the previous week. Obviously there had been the wedding, then the visit from the solicitor, another visit from a policeman, a statement given and witnessed, then nothing, until yesterday, when Hayden had told her they would be visiting his parents on the following day. She had felt scared, felt that she wanted to run away, to escape, but knew it was impossible. So, she had packed a small case, and when Hayden had told her to bring jeans and boots along with her padded jacket, she had added them to the dresses. And now they were in a plane heading towards Scotland, and she was going to meet her in-laws. Hayden had been good to her the week before. He had taken her out for a meal on a couple of occasions, not locally, but they had gone to restaurants away from the area, and eaten fantastic food and drunk good wine. They had talked, about anything and everything apart from themselves, and found they shared a love of books and music. She felt that it was almost as if he were courting her, but they were married already. She had found that Mrs. Bates, his housekeeper was as good as he said she was, she kept the house immaculate, and when she had offered her services, had been told that there was very little to do, apart from arrange the flowers that were delivered weekly, and a little light shopping in the nearby shops, if she would like to undertake that task, for she had help in the house from several people. Hayden had talked to her about money, giving her a good clothes allowance, but when she had protested, he had told her she could pay him back if she wanted to, when she had control of her finances again. There was very little physical contact between them, he would take her hand occasionally, but she knew that she was beginning to like him very much. She wondered if she would have ever known him, had he not visited her uncles' office. The stewardess bought them coffee, which they barely had time to drink, before they were coming into land, and as she had never liked the sensations which this engendered, she tensed, but suddenly Hayden was holding her hand, telling her that everything was alright, and there was nothing to worry about. She smiled at him, and muttered her thanks, then the plane was on the ground, and they had arrived. There were no customs to clear as this was an internal flight, and she found herself outside the terminal building, while Hayden looked around him, presumably for their transport to his parents' home. He hadn't told her exactly where it was, and she didn't like to question him too closely. But a large dark green Range Rover drew up, and a youngish man jumped out, and Hayden smiled at him, as they shook hands. "Hi, Hamish" he said. "I didn't know who would be meeting us, but I'm glad it's you. How are you?"

"Och, I'm fine Master Hayden. And this is your young lady wife?" He held out a hand to Deborah, and she took it, and had it shaken. "Hello Mistress Deborah." he said, "I'm Hamish. It's a pleasure to meet you." She began to relax, and watched as their luggage was stowed away in the boot of the car, and then she was ushered into the back seat. "Are you comfortable Debby?" Hayden asked. "It's going to be a long

journey," She nodded. "I'm fine thank you. How long is the journey going to be?"
Hamish turned in his seat. "Well, I left to collect you two hours ago, so providing we don't meet any hold ups, we should be home before tea time." Deborah wondered where they were going to go, but didn't say anything, and Hamish started the engine, and they were soon on their way. She didn't care much for the outskirts of Edinburgh, where they had landed, but the scenery soon changed, and she could see hills, covered in snow and heather, as they drove north eastwards. "The snow's early" Hayden said, and Hamish nodded. "Aye, it's not been too bad lower down, but we've had a few falls." They began to talk about the car, and Deborah lost interest in their conversation, just stared at the scenery. They began to climb, and the scenery got bleaker. There were fewer trees about now, apart from a few stands of timber along the road, but the colours of the hill side were glorious in a shaft of sunlight that suddenly appeared. The heather was purple, and mixed in were strands of yellow gorse. She gasped as she saw it, and failed to notice the smiling glance that Hayden shot at her. There were sheep on the hills now, along with a few cows, and she suddenly remembered being taken on a holiday with her parents, as a young girl to an Island, where the scenery had been similar. She couldn't remember where it was, and knew she'd have to look at the photo albums to remind herself of their journey. They had been driving for just over two hours now, and suddenly reached a wall that ran parallel to the road, and then turned onto a road at right angles to the road they were travelling on. Hamish swung the big car onto it,

and she saw a pair of impressive gates in the wall, either side of it. “Welcome home sir” he said quietly, and Hayden turned to see Deborah gazing at the gates. “We're nearly there Debby” he said. “Not too far to go now.” She nodded, and gazed around her. The car wound its way along the road, and finally reached another road, which they turned down. It ran straight for a good mile or so, and at its end, she could see a building – a house, no a castle! “Is that where we're going?” she asked and Hayden turned to see her. “Yes. It's a bit isolated, but its lovely. You'll like it, I hope”

“It's a castle” she said, and he grinned. “Not really, it's a fortified manor house. The earliest part of it was built in the 15th Century, and it’s been added onto at various times. It does have a few modern conveniences and central heating I'm pleased to say.”

“Aye, it could be a bit cold without any.” Hamish broke in, and Deborah stared as the house – no, castle – drew nearer. There were hills behind it, and she decided she liked the setting of the castle. Hamish swung the car round, to finish in the big gravelled area outside the front door, which opened to disgorge a man and a woman, and a dog, who was barking loudly. Hayden opened the car door, got out and embraced the woman who had flung herself at him, before he went to open Deborah's door, and escort her from the vehicle. “Mum” he said, as he drew Deborah to his side, “this is Debby. Debby, my parents” and he let her hand go, as he gave his father a hug. The dog was standing by his side now, had stopped barking, and instead was jumping up at him, and he bent and stroked it. “Bella, don't be daft.” he said quietly and the dog gave him an adoring look, and sat as close as it could to him. Deborah meanwhile was being greeted by Hayden's parents. “Hello Debby” his mother said quietly, and when Deborah would have held out a hand to be shaken, she was taken in the other woman's arms and given a big embrace. “Welcome to the family my dear” she said quietly. His father took over when his mother let her go, and looked at her. “Hello Debby. It's lovely to meet my new daughter-in-law.” and he too embraced her. “Hello” murmured Deborah, and Hayden grinned as he looked at her. “I think she's been overwhelmed. Let’s go inside and get warm. It's a bit fresh out here, isn't it?”, and he led the way to the front door, the dog keeping close to his side.

The hall of the house was massive – it had a vast stone staircase leading up from it to a gallery, which branched to reach both sides of the hall, and an enormous fireplace, in which a big log fire was burning. Hayden led them into a room on one side of the hallway, and as he ushered Debby in, she took a good look around her. The room was not much smaller than the hall, with a big log fire burning merrily, with three settees in a U shape in front of it. There were small tables nearby, and the whole room was lit by wall sconces around the walls. There was a vast chandelier in the centre of the room, but it was unlit, and the fire light was bouncing off it. The settees were of a light tweed tartan material, and the floor was covered in a darker carpet. There were a couple of cats curled up in the corner of one of the settees, a Siamese and a moggy, and they stretched as Hayden took Deborah's hand and bade her sit on the same settee, before he made himself comfortable next to the cats and began to stroke them. The dog who had been standing as close as possible to Hayden's legs, sat down beside him, and he stroked her ears, with the other hand. "You should have been a vet, not a doctor" his mother said with a laugh. "Now, are you very hungry, or do you want to go and see your room first Deborah? We'll never get Hayden to move now, that Bella and the cats have taken their opportunity to see him." and she laughed at her son, who was now being sat upon by the cats. "They adore him" she said, then smiled at her daughter-in-law. "Come with me my dear and I'll show your room, and you can get freshened up, and we can have a talk." and she led the way out of the room. Deborah heard his father say "No, leave them alone my boy," before she was led up the staircase to the gallery above. Her hostess turned left at the top of the stairs and led her to a door at the end of the gallery. "This will be your room" my dear, she said. "Hayden's is next door," and she indicated the door at right angles to her own. She opened the door and Deborah allowed herself to be ushered in. The room was big, but warm, and had a four-poster bed in it. "Wow" Deborah said as she looked at the bed. "I've never slept in a four-poster bed before Mrs Tomlinson." Hayden's mother sat in one of the easy chairs that were around the room. "Have a seat my dear, and we can have a chat, but please call me Eleanor, and my husband's David. Now, Hayden phoned us and told us everything, about you, your uncle and aunt, and the reason for your marriage." she sighed. "I hope that everything will soon be sorted out, and you'll have control of your father's company. But that's not what I wanted to say. I just wanted to tell you, that you'll always be welcome here

in this house, no matter what your reason is for marrying my son. I hope that in future," she stopped, then, "Well, let's just say, that I hope you'll be happy with Hayden my dear." she drew in a deep breath, and got up, to open a door. "This is your bathroom my dear, and there are plenty of wardrobes around. I'll leave you to settle in, and when you come downstairs again, then we can have tea about 4.00 pm. I ought to warn you that we eat heartily up here, and you could do with a bit more meat on your bones. But the other thing I wanted to tell you, is that my husband and myself, are the only people in this house who know the true reason why Hayden married you. There are quite a few people who live near here, who are going to wonder why you don't act as if you're in love while you're staying here. I'm sorry dear, but could you act the part? It won't be for too long, because I don't know when Hayden wants to leave, but I know he starts work on Monday morning, so he won't be saying too long." Deborah nodded. "I think I knew I'd have to act the part sometimes. I might as well try and get some practice in now. I hope Hayden doesn't mind me play acting."
"I don't think he will my dear. He will realise why you're doing it, especially as one of the people you are going to have to fool is his old Nanny. She can see through a block of wood, when it comes to Hayden. He could never get anything past her, when he was a boy." Deborah laughed with her hostess, and the older woman left the room. When she was alone, Deborah went into the bathroom, and found it was very modern, and contained everything she might need, including a range of make-up, combs, brushes, a vast

stack of towels, and little soaps. She grinned as she thought of having a bath in such a massive bath tub, before combing her hair, and tying it back again. The scar was very visible, and she inspected it, hoping it would soon fade a bit. When she was ready, she took a steadying breath, and went back to the room where she had left Hayden and his parents. The dog had wormed its way onto the settee, and was now lying with her head against one of his arms, and the cats were on his lap. "Okay?" he asked and she nodded, and went to sit near his mother. He and his father-in-law had been talking quietly, and she didn't want to interrupt their conversation, but nothing was said, and she began to be questioned by his mother. "How did you get on with my mother-in-law?" she asked, "She's an old tartar, but she's got a good heart." Deborah answered in a quiet manner, "Very well. She was good to me, and it turns out that she saw me when I was a babe in arms. My grandmother knew her when they were at school together, and apparently my mum and dad took me to see her before my grandmother passed away. She knew my dad as well, and was able to reminisce with me about him." Hayden's mother nodded. "She told me that she knew your father, but didn't mention she'd seen you when you were so young." She grinned "What about Estelle? She came here to be a cook, but she got on so well with Lady Grimes, when she visited, she asked her to become her companion. I think they're so in tune with each other now, they'll never change."

"She's very nice as well. They were the witnesses at our wedding you know?"

"So, what did you wear my dear? Typical men, can't

describe anything even when it's in front of their noses. I did ask Hayden, but all he could tell me was that it was a blue dress."

"It wasn't a dress" she said, and Hayden lifted his head to look at her in shock. "Wasn't it? I thought it was." She shook her head. "It was a pale blue suit, in a wool mix material. It had a fitted jacket, and a flared skirt. I had a white silk blouse on underneath the jacket, and my hair was loose, because I wanted to hide my scar as much as possible." and she showed her mother-in-law the scar by her eye. "I can't get over how badly he could have injured you" Eleanor looked closely at the scar. "Did Hayden sew it up?" she asked, and when Deborah nodded, she looked at her son and smiled. "Not a bad job of stitchery" she said, with a hint of mischief.

"Not bad?" he cried, "I'll have you know that I was congratulated on my stitching by the casualty officer at the hospital, who inspected it, when I took Debby into the A&E department."

"Did he know who you were?" she asked, mystifying Deborah, but Hayden shook his head. "He didn't have a clue" he said. He looked around him. "Bella's here, but where's Tilda? She normally comes and sees me the moment I get home."

"She's out in the whelping pen" his father told him. "Her litter are due to go to their new homes soon, and she's having a last few days with them. I think she'll be pleased to see them go, there were six and we've found homes for all but one. He was the runt of the litter, but he's got a bit of a temper on him, and he hasn't been picked by anybody who came to see him, because he snaps and snarls at them, and puts them

off, so he spends quite a lot of time with his mother." he looked over at Deborah. "You'll see her tomorrow, when we show you around the grounds."
They carried on talking, until the door opened, and an elderly lady bought in a tray of tea and cakes. She placed it on the table, then came across to the settee, where Hayden was sitting. "Hello Master Hayden" she said, and bent and kissed him on the cheek. "Nanny," he cried. "More beautiful than ever."
"Go on with you." the old lady said. "You always could charm the birds off the trees. But its lovely to see you again."
"Nanny, this is Deborah, my wife" Hayden said, and Deborah got up to shake hands with the woman. She was conscious of being inspected by the old Nanny, and finally she smiled, and ignoring the hand, bent and kissed her on the cheek. "You're welcome, my dear." she said. "I hope you'll be very happy with Master Hayden. He's a good boy really."
"It's nice to meet you Miss...?" but Nanny interrupted, "Call me Nanny my dear. Everybody does." She looked at Eleanor. "Shall I pour Mrs. T.?" and when Eleanor nodded, the old lady did just that, and the atmosphere and the talk in the room became very jolly.

When Deborah left the lounge that evening, after dinner, she found Eleanor by her side. Hayden's mother patted her hand. "You did very well, my dear." she said softly. "Nanny was convinced. She told me that she's delighted that Hayden has found himself such a lovely young woman, who obviously thinks the world of him. But you do know you're going to have to continue with the charade until you leave here?

Hayden was acting well also, so I'm proud of the pair of you. Now, you just get along to bed, and I'll see you in the morning. Mrs. Drew will bring you a cup of tea in bed, and we'll see you at breakfast." and she watched as Deborah went up the stairs to her room.

The following day when she awoke, she got out of bed and went to look out of the window. The weather had turned, and it was raining, but she saw that the moorland looked just as lovely as it had done the day before, and she wondered if she would be able to go for a walk. There was a tap at the door, and the housekeeper came in with a tray of tea. "Mrs. Tomlinson asked me to bring you a cup" she said, as she placed it on the bedside table. "She said to tell you breakfast will be served in an hour's time."

"Thank you very much." Deborah replied, as she sat on the edge of the bed, and watched as the housekeeper left the room. It was nearly an hour later, and she was almost ready to leave the room, when there was a tap on the door, and she called "come in," wondering as she did so, who it was. She was totally unprepared to see Hayden enter. He came across to her, and looked at her. "You look as though you had a really good night's sleep" he said. "I was wondering if you wanted to come for a walk later on. It's drizzling a bit, but I think it will stop soon, and you could get some fresh air, and I know you like walking." She smiled at him. "I'd love to. Will it be okay if I get changed after breakfast, or shall I change now?"

"After breakfast will be fine. I thought I'd ask now, as Nanny will want to know what we'll be up to all day. We can take the dogs with us. Are you ready to go

down? If so, we can go together."
She nodded. "I'm ready, so let's go." and she stood up. He took her hand, and escorted her from the room. She was glad he had done so, when she saw Nanny watching them from the hall, as they left her room together, and go downstairs. "Morning Nanny" she said, with a broad smile, and the old lady smiled back. "Morning Miss Debby and you too Master Hayden. What are you going to do today?" She saw Hayden smile, and knew he was amused that his old Nanny had done exactly what she had done as he had predicted. "We're going to go for a walk with the dogs." she said. "Hayden said he is going to show me all his favourite spots." Hayden squeezed her hand. "Aren't I lucky to have found somebody who likes the countryside as much as I do?" he asked, as they reached the bottom and he escorted her into the dining room. "You're a lucky young man Master Hayden" she said, and went on her way to the kitchen. "Thanks" he muttered, as he opened the door, and she smiled up at him. She had discovered it wasn't hard playing the loving wife, for she did like him, more than she had ever liked anybody before, and wondered if he found the play acting difficult. She didn't bother to think any more about that, but instead greeted her host and hostess, and got on with her breakfast.

She had changed her clothes, and carried her boots downstairs, along with her waterproof jacket, and met Hayden in the hallway. "Almost ready?" he asked, and she sat down to put her walking boots on. She stood up, put her coat on and stood up, said "ready" and he took her hand. "Come on, let's go and get the dogs."

and led her out the front door. Bella, the Shetland sheepdog was standing ready, and her father-in-law was talking to Hamish. "We'll go and get Tilda" he said. "She might be glad of a long walk after looking after the puppies."
"Aye" said Hamish, "they'll be going soon, and she could do with a break. She'll only have the wee one left, unless we can find somebody who wants it."
Hayden led her across the courtyard behind the house, and they entered a stable block. There were several horses in the stalls – one a huge bay Shire, with a black mane and tail, enormous white feet, and next to it, was a Suffolk Punch, as well as two riding horses, a large dark bay belonging to his father and a smaller grey, for his mother. "We still like to use horses to do some of the work on the estate. They're better for the environment, than tractors" Hayden said, as he rubbed the nose of the Shire. "This is Derinda, and the Suffolk Punch is Zeus." The two horses were gorgeous, and she was soon patting their necks and stroking their coats. "I like this one best" she said, patting the Shire mare, and he grinned. "She was a champion and she's in foal to one of the best stallions in the country, so we're hoping that the foal will be as good as its mother. But Zeus is in foal as well, and as there are so few Suffolk Punches left, every foal is precious. They won't be working now until after the foals are born, and they are both due in February. Everybody is pleased they're both so well. Lots of people like to have them, despite the fact that they're so big. I think Dad would like to breed them, and I know he's considering getting another one or two Suffolks soon, to try and increase their numbers. Come and see Tilda and the puppies"

and he led the way to the whelping pen. Tilda was another Shetland sheep dog, and she was surrounded by five bouncy puppies, but the sixth, the littlest one, a blue merle, was curled up for sleep. Deborah was stroking Tilda, and the dog obviously loved the attention she was getting, before Hayden bent and picked up the smallest puppy. "Watch it Master Hayden!" Hamish said. "He's not got the best temper of a puppy." Hayden grinned at him. "Don't worry about it. He seems to be quite docile at the moment." He stroked the puppy, who growled and wriggled in an effort to be put down. "This is the runt of the litter, and the only one who hasn't been snapped up" he said, and put him into Deborah's arms. The puppy yawned, opened his eyes, then licked her wrist and cuddled against her. "Oh, he's beautiful" she said, stroking him. The puppy licked her wrist again, and snuggled close to her, closed his eyes, then yawned, and went to sleep again. Hayden looked at her, and the puppy and realised they were made for each other. "Would you like him?" he asked, and she stared at him. "For my very own?" she said, and he nodded. "Please" she said, "but only if your parents don't object. I could take him for long walks and train him, couldn't I?" Hayden nodded again. "Okay, put him down now, and we'll take his mum and Bella for a walk, and you can come and see him again this afternoon." She did as she had been told, and as she put him down again, the puppy licked her hand. She patted him goodbye, and stood up. Hamish was staring at the puppy. "He's never behaved like that with anybody else" he said wonderingly, and turned away to go to give the horses some attention. Deborah smiled at her husband

"Thank you Hayden" she said, and reached up to kiss him on the cheek. He turned at the last minute, so that his lips met hers, and he kissed her. He put her away from him, with a curious expression on his face, and she drew in a deep breath. There was silence for a minute, then, "Come on" he said. "Let's go for that walk" and he opened the pen door for her to exit. Tilda came with them, and he shut it firmly behind him, to stop the other puppies trying to leave. Tilda seemed to be delighted to be away from her puppies, and she and Bella scampered off together. "This way" he said, and took her hand, and led her away from the house. They walked for miles, with the dogs running to and fro before them, while they talked about nothing in particular. The time passed quickly, and she began to enjoy herself greatly, as they walked. He told her of the estate, and its size, and the number of people who lived on it, and she asked question after question about the plants and the birds around. They were on their way back to the house, when they caught up with an elderly woman, carrying a basket on her hip. "Hello Maggie" Hayden said, and the old woman turned and her face broke into a smile as she saw who it was. "Master Hayden" she said, "oh its lovely to see you again. And who's this?" she asked, as she eyed Deborah. "This is my wife, Deborah" he introduced her. "Debby this is Maggie McKendrick. She's the wife of one of our old shepherds and they live in a cottage down near the house. Maggie had 8 children, and they all went to school with my sisters and I."

"Eight children?" Deborah said round eyed, and the old woman looked at her. "Aye" she said. "They're grand kids, and I'm proud of them all. I've got 16 grandchildren now as well, and two more on the way, and I expect more when my youngest gets married next year."

"Congratulations" they both said, and Hayden continued, "we've just been for a long walk with the dogs, and Mother will be expecting us for lunch, so we'd better be getting on our way."

"Just a minute Master Hayden. I'd like to have a look at Miss Deborah's hand" and she took Deborah's right hand in hers, and held it, as she peered at it. "Trouble" she said, "trouble but happiness as well, but the ecstasy will be delayed, but it will come. But the trouble will come again. But I can see that the Little One will help. Aye, definitely the Little One." and she let her hand go, then passed her hand across her eyes. "I'm sorry" she said simply. "I shouldn't have done that" She turned away. "Stay well, and stay away from that man" she said. "Goodbye" and she was gone, swiftly walking down a different path to the one they were on. Deborah turned to see Hayden staring after the old woman. "What did she mean?" she asked, but Hayden shook his head. "She's got the second sight, and some of her pronunciations sound very strange to us. But I've never known her wrong." he sighed and looked at the dogs, patiently waiting for them. "Come on, we'll be so late for lunch and Nanny will scold us." he grinned, took her hand and hurried her down to the house.

"We've found a home for the little puppy" Hayden said at lunchtime. "If you don't mind, Debby would like it please." His mother smiled, and nodded. "We wondered if you would like him" she said. "He's a

sweetheart, but nobody else seemed to want him. If somebody came to view him, he would snap and growl at them, try to bite them, and they changed their minds. But I'm so glad that he's found a home now."
"Funny" said Hayden, "Hamish warned me about him as well, and he did growl at me but I picked him up, put him in Debby's arms, and he licked her, cuddled up against her and went to sleep in her arms. He obviously accepted her immediately." His father smiled at them. "Well, if he and Debby are going to be friends, then I'm sure we don't mind him going with you." Deborah had smiled at him. "Thank you" she said simply. "I'm sure he's going to be my friend." They had eaten their meal, and the conversation had changed. They were having coffee after lunch, when Hayden told his parents that they had met up with Maggie, and told them what she had said, and his mother looked at him. "What exactly did she say?" she asked, and Deborah told her all that she remembered of the words. "What does that mean?" she asked, but Eleanor shook her head. "Goodness knows. But remember she does know what she's talking about. Maybe she means that your uncle is going to try and cause more problems for you and that's what she means by trouble. But the Little One? That one I can't work out." Hayden smiled at his parent. "We'll let you know" he said simply, and with that they had to be content. That afternoon, he had to go with Hamish to collect his new car, and although he asked Deborah if she wanted to go with him, she refused, she wanted to think about the morning. He had told Hamish and Sam, the stable manager, that he and Deborah would be having the little puppy, and that afternoon, Deborah

went out to the whelping pen to see him and the horses, again. She had pulled forward an old metal box and was sitting on it, with the puppy laying in her arms, nuzzling her hand, when she heard a step behind her, and looked up to see David, Hayden's father standing in the doorway. "He's beautiful" she said, "and he's not really much smaller than the others, is he? Will he always be smaller than the others of his litter?"

"No, he'll probably grow quite quickly, once he's on his own. He's really taken to you, hasn't he? He never behaved like that, when anybody else came to see him. I think you two were probably destined for each other. I think Hayden will be delighted to have him in the house for you. It will give you something to look after and care for when Hayden's busy with his job. But I wanted to ask you something, lassie. I know why you married Hayden, but are you feeling happier than you were? He seems to think you need time to yourself occasionally, and that's why you wanted to be alone on your wedding day, but do you think you could be happy with him? He's a good man, even if I do say so, as his father, and I'd like you to be content with your lot."

"Yes, I think I could be happy" she said, and knew as she said it, that she could be. "I did need time for myself on our wedding day. I think I just needed to get out and have a breath of fresh air. Even when I was working for my uncle, I'd be able to get some fresh air, and be alone for a bit, when I walked home from the office, and that helped me. And I wanted to think about things as well." she smiled at her father-in-law. "This morning, we had a lovely walk, and that was what I needed to relax me. When he's older, I'll be able to take this one for long walks in some of the parks near where Hayden lives, and get some fresh air in me, which will help and relax me, I'm sure."

"I'm glad" he said. "If you ever need to get away, you can always visit us here. You can fly up and somebody will meet you at the airport, or you could drive up, if Hayden can't get away from the hospital."

"No, I couldn't" she said. "I've never learnt to drive a car, and I don't have access to one."

"Can you not?" he said. "Hayden might not be the best person to teach you then, maybe you'd better get a course of lessons and you could surprise him one day. And of course, he'll buy you a car if you want one."

"I don't really think so" she said with a grin. "But learning to drive would be a big surprise for him, wouldn't it?"

"That it would, lass, that it would" he drew in a deep breath. "Anyway, tea will be on the table soon, and we'd better not be late for it. Hayden will be late getting back, it's a long drive, and he'll be taking it steady." She gave the puppy a final hug, put him back in the pen, promised to see him again, and pushed the box back where she had found it, and she and her father-in-law walked back to the house together.

Chapter Five

Hayden arrived home late that evening, and came into the lounge where everybody was waiting for him. "Everything okay?" his father asked, and he nodded. "It's a very nice car – bigger than my Volvo, but it drives like a dream, and it's just what I've been looking for. I can't believe I managed to get it from somebody who lives near here." he turned to Deborah, and explained. "I've been trying to find one of these cars for a long time, and I'd put an agent onto it, and he found one near Edinburgh. The guy who'd ordered it, didn't like it when he got it, so he put it up for sale, and I managed to acquire it. You can see it tomorrow."

"Have you eaten?" his mother asked, and he nodded. "Hamish and I stopped for a bite to eat on the way back, and we did some shopping as well. Debby's puppy needed a carrier in which to travel, so I got one on the way. What are you going to call him?" he asked her, with a smile, but she shook her head. "I've got no idea. I spent some time with him and his mother this afternoon, but all the names I thought of, don't seem to suit him." she grinned, "I can have fun thinking of something on the drive back." She looked up at her husband's face "How long is the drive back going to take? If it took nearly two hours to get here from the airport, it's going to take a lot longer to get back to your house."

"You're right, and that's why we'll have to leave very soon after an early breakfast tomorrow. I'm sorry it was only a short visit Mum, but you'll be able to come and see us before Christmas, won't you? Maybe some of the girls can come and visit at the same time." His mother nodded. "I don't think Sandra will be able to come. She'll be too near her due date at Christmas, but Katrina might be able to visit." Deborah sat quietly thinking about Hayden and his family. He had told her that he had four sisters, Sandra, the eldest, lived in Northumberland, had two children already and was expecting her third in the New Year, Katrina lived with her husband in Kent and didn't have any children yet, Patricia lived in Essex, and had two children, and the youngest Lucy, lived with her new husband in Edinburgh, but had been away this weekend, so she hadn't met any of them. She wondered what it would be like to have a large family. She had been an only child, and although she had been happy with her parents, she knew she had missed out on having siblings when she was growing up. "Debby?" her husband's voice broke into her musings, and she turned her face to him. "Sorry, did you say something?" she asked, and he smiled at her. "Just wondered if you wanted anything to drink?" he said. "I was getting something for mum and dad, and I wondered if you wanted anything?"

"Can I have a glass of port please?" she smiled at his expression. "I quite like it. I'd never tried it before, but I had some when I was staying with your grandmother, and it's quite nice." He nodded, and went over to the drink's cabinet, and soon came back with a glass which he handed to her, and sat beside her on the settee. "So, what did you do this afternoon?" he asked her softly, and she shrugged. "I went out to see the horses again, and then sat and played with all the puppies, before I gave my puppy a big cuddle. There was a nice man in the stable, and he let me give Derinda and Zeus an apple each. And he took them out for a run in the field, and later, he let me help him bring them back to the stable."

"That would be Sam." her husband told her. "He looks after the horses and the dogs, despite the fact that the dogs normally live in the house when they aren't busy having puppies. The cats like going out to be with the horses as well, but only when they're not inside being lazy." and he stroked the Siamese cat that had come to sit with them. "Sam started work on the estate when my grandfather was alive, and he's made his life here. I think he thinks that the horses belong to him."

"He was nice to me. He let me stroke them and showed me how to groom them. He showed me all the ribbons they've won in the shows. They've got loads of them, haven't they?" He nodded, then said "Were you bored on your own?" She shook her head. "No, I like being on my own sometimes, I told your father that, when he came to get me for tea."

"I think you'll have plenty of time to be on your own when we're back home" he said quietly. "I think my job might entail me having to spend quite a bit of time in the hospital, so I won't be able to be with you, but I hope you won't mind too much." She shook her head. "No, I can find things to do, and now I'll have the puppy to look after and train. I'll have to get a book on how to do it."

"Don't bother, I've got a couple at home, and you can read those." She thanked him, and smiled at his father, when he came to sit with them. "Go and talk to your mother Hayden" he said. "She's always saying she doesn't see enough of you, and as you'll have to leave early in the morning, I think she will want to have a chat." Hayden agreed, and went to sit by his mother's side. They started talking quietly together, and as they were on the other side of the fire, Deborah couldn't hear what was being said. "Did anybody show you round the house?" his father asked, and she shook her head. "No, not really."

"Well, come and I'll show you around. When you come again, you'll be able to see more of it, but you can have a quick look now." He stood up, and announced "I'm going to give Debby a quick look at the house. We'll be back later on." and ushered Deborah out into the hall. "So, that side obviously is the lounge, you've seen the dining room, and here we have my study and the library." He opened another door and Deborah entered the library. It was a large room, lined with bookshelves reaching the ceiling, with ladders attached to enable reaching the top shelf, and several small tables, each with its own lamp, and easy chair. "Have you read all these?" she asked and he grinned at her, looking so much like his son, that she felt at ease. "Good gracious no!" he said. "Some of these books haven't been opened since my great grandfather put them on the shelves. Most of our light reading is down this end," and he led the way to shelves which contained the latest thrillers, as well as other books on sheep and horse breeding, as well as management of cattle all mixed in with romances or reference books. "We really ought to classify everything" he said, "but both Eleanor and I know where things are, so we just keep it like it is. The children come in here to read, and we've got loads of books for them." and he showed her the shelves. Some of the books on them were old, and she was surprised when David told her that some of them had belonged to her husband when he was a boy. She looked at the titles, and then remembered some of the books that her parents had bought for her, when she was younger, and which had been thrown out by her uncle. “I had some of these when I was a child” she said, swallowing tears. “My uncle threw them out when he and aunty moved into my house. He called them childish rubbish, and said they weren't needed any more.” David put an arm around her shoulders, and gave her a hug. “Books are never rubbish” he declared. “In fact, I think there are a few here, that belonged to me, and my sisters. Don't worry Debby, Hayden will help you and your solicitor, to get back what belongs to you.”

“It's not the possessions that worry me, they've gone forever,” she said, “it’s the fact that my uncle thought he could treat me like a servant, while having taken everything from me. I'm hoping that Mr. Rickards will be able to get some of the money back, because I owe it to Hayden. He's bought me loads of clothes, and I owe him for them.”

“Just accept them Debby” he gave her a hug again. “I think he's enjoying spending some of his ill-gotten gains on somebody besides himself. He does have another income apart from what he earns you know.”

“Yes, he told me that, but he spent so much on me. I don't want to be in so much debt to him.”

“Don't worry about it my dear. Now, let’s go and see some more of the house” and he led her away. There were many other rooms on the ground floor, but the kitchen, when they reached it, was massive, having an Aga stove, and a big Belfast sink, but it was also equipped with every modern item, any woman could desire. The housekeeper was sitting at the kitchen table, reading a newspaper. “I thought you'd have gone up to the flat?” David said, but she shook her head. “I went up there, remembered I'd left my glasses down here, started reading the paper and got engrossed in this item about some people I know.” Her father-in-law nodded. “I'm just showing Deborah round the house. She and Hayden will be leaving early in the morning, and she hasn't had a chance to see round it yet.”

Deborah looked around her. “It's a beautiful kitchen” she said. “Do you have any help in the kitchen and house, for the food was incredible, and the house is kept so beautiful, I can't believe you manage on your own.”

“Well thank you very much Miss Deborah. I do have lots of help, and I enjoy cooking. I hear you're a good cook as well.”

“I did a French cookery course while I was at school, and I enjoyed learning how to cook things. I haven't had much chance to cook anything for the last few weeks.” The housekeeper nodded. “I expect Master Hayden's housekeeper will let you loose in the kitchen if you want to cook” she said. David had been standing by, but now he spoke. “Come on then Debby, you haven't seen anything of upstairs yet, and there's lots to see.” Deborah said goodbye to the housekeeper, and David led her out of the kitchen, and up the staircase. “You've obviously seen your room, and Hayden's room is next door and similar to yours, and there are plenty of spare rooms on this floor. The rooms over there” and he indicated a set of double doors on the other side of the gallery "they're mine and Eleanor's, and then if we go down this passage, we'll find the staircase to the next floor." He led her up a small staircase, and she found herself on another landing, which had several doors in it. "These are all bedrooms" he said, "and they get used whenever the rest of the family come." He then took her up another flight of stairs and opened a door at the top. "This is the children's play room" he said, and she stared around her in envy. There was a massive doll's house on one low table, and she looked inside it and found that it contained everything that a young child could want. There was a train set, on a board, with tunnels, stations, and she could imagine boys playing with it. "The trains are kept separately" he said. "Hayden and his cousin Jack would play with it for hours, and if I could spare the time, then I'd come and play with it as well." and he laughed with her. "I adored trains when I was younger. Mother always said I'd become a train driver." He showed her the cupboards full of children's toys and she could have spent hours in there, just looking. "We keep everything ready for when our grandchildren come and visit. They like spending time in here. There are smaller rooms up here for them especially and there are other rooms for the children's nurses, and then another couple of guest rooms. On the floor above the kitchen, there's a big flat which we made for Mrs. Drew, which is accessible from the kitchen, and a smaller flat for the girls who help her. Because we're so isolated, we felt it would be easier for them to have their own space. And then there are the attics, but I'm not taking you up there. Two of the turrets have space in them which are bedrooms, but they're not often used, and the other turrets have storage rooms in them." He stopped talking, and smiled. "And that's basically the house. Its big, but we do have a big family, and when we all get together, we need the space." He led the way out of the playroom, and went down the stairs to the gallery again. "You can imagine what fun my sisters and I had when I was a child living here. I only hope that my children had as much fun as I did."

"Yes, we did" said Hayden from the staircase, where he had stood listening to their conversation. "I came up to find out where you were. Mum thought the ghost might have got you."

"What ghost?" Deborah asked startled, and the two men laughed. "There's a rumour that this place is haunted, but we've never seen it," said Hayden. David was laughing, but he stopped now, and said, "Don't forget what Maggie McKendrick says about this place. She's convinced that the White Lady will appear when there's danger to a member of the family." He shook his head. "I like Maggie, but she says things sometimes, that I don't know how to take. When you and Debby met her his morning for example. I know she's got second sight, but I wish her predictions made sense and not riddles." They had gone downstairs as they had been speaking, and as they entered the lounge, Eleanor looked up. "I thought the White Lady had got you" she laughed. Her husband smiled at her as he came to sit beside her. "No, Debby and I were fascinated by the play room. I think you'd better bring her back soon Hayden, and she can spend time there and play with the doll's house to her heart's content."

Deborah laughed and thanked Hayden as he handed

her the drink he had poured for her, and which she hadn't finished. “It's a lovely house” she said. “Thank you for showing me round it.” The talk became general, and as the room was warm, and she'd had a lot of exercise that day, Deborah found herself yawning. “Would anybody mind if I went to bed?” she said. “It's been a long day, but I've really enjoyed myself.” Hayden stood up and came to her. “Not in the least. I'll see you in the morning” he said, and waited while she said good night to his relatives. He opened the door for her, and when she said goodnight, he bent and kissed her on the cheek. “Goodnight Debby. Sleep well” he said, and kissed her again, this time on the lips. She looked at him, not wanting to say anything, then with an effort, said “goodnight” and ran up the stairs to her room. She shut the door behind her, wondering why he had kissed her, for they had had little physical contact before they visited his parents, then she smiled to herself. Nanny would have been somewhere about, she thought, and Hayden wanted to preserve the image in the old woman's eyes. She had a swift bath, got ready for bed, and turning out the lights, she slept.

The following morning, Hayden came to her room to escort her downstairs to breakfast, and she felt the pressure of his hand on hers increase, as Nanny watched them come down the staircase together. “When will you be going?” she asked Hayden, “I've hardly seen you, and I haven't had any chance to have a chat to Miss Deborah.”

“Sorry Nanny, we'll be going as soon as we've eaten. It's a long drive, and we'll have to have a few stops on

the way, to see that the puppy is alright."
"Aye, I heard you were going to have the puppy. Well, when you come again, promise me you'll have a long talk with me." the old woman demanded, and Hayden leant forward to kiss her on the cheek. "I promise Nanny" he said. "We'll come and see you especially, and you can cross-examine Debby to your heart's content." he grinned at both women, before he took Deborah's hand "Come on Debby, breakfast" and he led her into the dining room.

She had packed her clothes into her bag, and taken everything downstairs, when Hayden came into the hallway. "Let's go and get the puppy" he said, as he picked up her bag and waterproof coat. He led her outside and she gasped as she saw the car standing majestically on the driveway in front of the house. It was a Bentley Flying Spur motor, and he grinned as he saw her face. "I thought it was great when I first had a ride in one, and I've been wanting to get my hands on one for a long time." he said and opened the boot to put her case in. He took from there, a large animal carrier, and handed her a harness and lead. "I'll let you put them on him. He won't be able to go out for a while, until he's had his injections, you know that don't you?" and she nodded, as they made their way through the archway to the back of the house, and the stables. Sam was waiting for them, and Hayden stopped to talk to him. Deborah went through to the stables, and saw the horses waiting for them. She patted them, said her goodbyes, and carried on to the stall where the whelping pen was. Standing by it, she saw the same little old lady, she had seen the day

before. “Hello” she said and the woman nodded. “We're going home today, and I'm going to take the puppy with me.” The woman nodded again, and Hayden said behind her “Who are you talking to Debby?” She turned to see him, then indicated the old lady, but when she turned round again, there was nobody there. “Oh, one of the ladies who works in the house, I think.” she said. “I saw her yesterday as well, but she didn't speak then, just smiled at me.”
“Sam, who's been coming in to see the puppies?” Hayden asked, as the other man joined them. “Most of the house staff” he said, “as well as a few from the cottages” and he indicated a row of houses a distance from the house. “What did she look like Debby?” Hayden asked, and she shrugged. “Oh, just a little old lady, wearing an enormous white apron, over a print dress. She looked as if she were from another century, if you know what I mean?” Hayden nodded, then exchanged glances with Sam, but Deborah didn't notice, for she was bending down in front of the whelping pen. Her puppy was bouncing around the pen, but came towards her when he saw her, “You'll have to call him Bouncer if he keeps on springing around like that” Hayden said with a smile, but Deborah shook her head. “No, I don't think so. I'll think of something. Sam opened the pen door, and bent down to stroke all the puppies and Tilda. “Say goodbye to your little one” he said to the dog, and picked up the puppy, who growled at him. “Oh, stop it” he said quietly, as he held it towards its mother's nose, which it licked, then as the puppy continued to growl, he shook his head, and handed it to Deborah. The puppy stopped growling, and instead licked

Deborah's hand, and she cuddled it close to her, and stroked it. "You can see how he reacted to anybody else who came to see him" Sam said, and Hayden nodded. "I think he knows that Debby is going to be special to him" he replied, then turned his attention to Deborah who was cuddling the puppy, and not taking any notice of the two men. "Can you put his harness on him for me please" she said to Hayden, "I don't think I'd be able to manage it on my own." Hayden nodded, took the harness from her, and fastened it around the puppy's body. Deborah opened the carrier, and he put the puppy inside, on a couple of old towels and a blanket. He grinned and reached into the bedding and produced a small teddy bear, which he put in with the puppy. "He might be lonely, without any playmates, and that will smell of his mum and his siblings. We put one in the pen for each puppy, and they go with them when they go to their new homes." he said, as Deborah shut the door. "Bye bye Tilda," she said, patting the bitch. "I'll look after your baby for you", and she carried the pet carrier to the door, and out of the stable block. The puppy was placed on the back seat of the car, and the carrier belted into place, and people were appearing to say their farewells. Deborah went to say goodbye to Nanny and the housekeeper and thank them for the delicious meals that had been served, before saying her farewells to Hayden's mother and father. "Thank you for making me welcome" she said to Eleanor. "I did enjoy myself."

"You must come again soon" Eleanor said, giving her a hug, "and we'll be coming to stay with either you or my mother-in-law before Christmas, so we'll see you then. Take care of yourself my dear, and I hope things got sorted very soon."

"So do I" Deborah said with feeling, and Eleanor laughed. Her husband was speaking to his son, and he shot a glance at Deborah, but Hayden shook his head, and said nothing, "Goodbye Debby" his father said, kissing her on the cheek. "See you soon." Hayden opened the car door for her, and she slid down into the seat. "Oh, my goodness" she said, "it's like getting into a bed" Hayden laughed, as he shut the door, and went round to get into the driver's seat. Everybody was waving, and Deborah said quietly, "There's that lady again Hayden" she pointed, but the woman had gone. "Probably left a pan on the stove, and just remembered it" he said, with a grin. "Ready to go?" She nodded and he started the engine, and waved as he set off on their long journey. Deborah waved until the car turned a corner and she couldn't see the house any more. She turned in her seat to see if the puppy was alright, and found that he had gone to sleep in his carrier, one paw across the teddy bear. "I thought puppies had a lot more energy than he seems to have" she said, and Hayden laughed. "Oh, he'll be lively enough in the future, you can bank on it. He probably wore himself out this morning having a romp with his brothers and sisters. He'll wake again soon. We'll have to have a few stops so he can stretch his legs." He carried on talking as he drove along the road they had arrived on, until he turned onto the major road, and increased speed. "So, what did you think of my parents?" he asked and she smiled as she remembered. "They were incredibly nice to me, and they made me feel very welcome. Do they come and stay with you frequently?"

"Well, they would go and visit grandmother occasionally, before I moved to be near her, and as our house is large enough, they can stay either with me, or with her. Dad visits fairly frequently, as he sometimes has to see people about the estate, and he catches up with his friends, but Mum only comes down to go shopping a couple of times a year. And of course, I visit from time to time. I think they regret the fact that the girls and I are so far from them, but they've never said anything. Of course, they go and see Lucy and Sandra fairly frequently, as Lucy only lives about two hours' drive and Sandra's a bit further on about four hours' drive from them."
"Is this the way we came when we arrived?" she asked, for she didn't recognise anything of the landscape, but he shook his head. "No, this is the quickest way. If you fly and land at Edinburgh, there is only one main road through to the estate, but we're going the other way. We'll join the motorway in a while, and then it will be a boring drive to home, I'm afraid. Quick but boring. I meant to ask you, if you'd ever been to Scotland before? You didn't say anything, and I wondered."
"I can't really remember, because I was quite young when we went." she admitted. "I know we went to an Island somewhere, for I can remember we had to go on a ferry, and I remember that the hillsides were like the ones we passed on the way up, so we might have visited the Highlands. I know there are some photos in one of the albums, so I can have a look and see if they're labelled." She gestured around her, at the scenery they were passing through, "I think these colours are fantastic, purple and yellow, and all of the different spectrums of the two colours. Mix that in

with the white of the sheep and the different colour cows on the hillside, and it's a fantastic combination of colours." Hayden shot her a glance, and smiled. "I'm glad you like it" he said. "I can't take the credit for it, but I'm glad it's pleased you." She laughed at his words and the journey continued.

They had reached the motorway, and Hayden let the car speed up, and she was enjoying the envious looks that the car was getting. They had gone across the border into England, when they had to slow as the weather started to become bad. "I hadn't thought about this" he muttered. "I think I'll turn off somewhere, and we can have a break, and let the pup stretch his legs." He took the next turn off, and they carried on a minor road for some while, until he drew up in front of a pub. "I think coffee is called for" he said, and undid the belt holding the carrier in place. He opened the door, clipped the lead on, and allowed the puppy to exit the carrier. A couple of minutes' walk, was all he allowed, but as he said, "the puppy isn't vaccinated yet, and as he's got a long journey, he only needs a little exercise to stop him getting too tired in the carrier." He put him back in the crate, gave him a drink, and ushered Deborah into the pub, where the landlord was only too willing to let them have a hot drink. The lady who bought their drinks, looked into the carrier, and broke into a smile. "Oh, isn't he gorgeous?" she said. "What's the little one's name?" Deborah and Hayden shared a smile, as Deborah replied, "he hasn't got one yet. We've only just got him, and I can't think what he should be called." The lady smiled at them both. "First pet?" she asked, and

Deborah nodded. “Well, good luck to you both,” she said, and went back to her work. Deborah drank her coffee, and made her way to the Ladies room, where she tidied herself, before going back to where Hayden was waiting for her. “I've had a word with the landlord, and he reckons we should get going, because there's bad weather heading this way. Apparently, it’s been very bad in the South, and it’s on its way up country. Shall we get going?” he asked and she nodded. They called goodbye to the people in the pub, and went out to the car, where Hayden put the puppy carrier back inside, and Deborah got into the front seat again. “This car is a lot heavier than my last one” he said, “and if the wind is going to be very strong, I think I'm going to be glad of it.” He put the car into gear and they set off again, and headed back towards the motorway. After that, the journey took on a nightmare quality to Deborah. The sky was the colour of a deep bruise, and the wind was blowing hard. The rain that fell was so heavy that the motorway speed was restricted, but despite that, Deborah could see cars racing past them, “Idiots” Hayden growled, as they were passed by two cars, going well above the speed limit. “I hate boy racers and those two are an accident waiting to happen” He slowed his speed further as the rain became even heavier, and visibility was limited, but there was nowhere to go, other than onwards. They hadn't passed an exit for a while, and he was busy concentrating on the road ahead, and not talking. Deborah didn't really want to talk anyway, she was holding tight to her handbag strap, wanting to have something in her hands, and she gasped, as Hayden put his hand on hers. "Relax Debby" he said. "You'll be

quite safe, I promise you."
"I know that" she said, "I trust you, but I've never really liked storms and this is one of the worse I've ever been in." He laughed at her words. "If there's an accident, and we have to stop, promise me you won't get out. Stay here, and you'll be safe."
"I promise," she said, and he squeezed her hands again. "Good girl" he said quietly, and put both hands on the wheel again. The traffic had been slowing, but now it came to a halt, and he shook his head. "I think there's been an accident" he said, "and we could be held up here for a while. I'll find out if there's anything I can do. Remember, stay inside and you'll be safe." He had pulled the car onto the hard shoulder, along with several others, and he reached into the back for his waterproof jacket. "I'll be back" he said, kissed her fiercely on her surprised mouth, and he opened the door and got out, and walked across to where a policeman was controlling traffic. Deborah could see him talking, then he was back at the car. "I'm just getting my bag. I won't be long" he said, closed the door and he was gone again. Time passed fairly slowly, the puppy was still sleeping, and she didn't even have him to talk to, and she was wondering where Hayden was, when he was at the door, putting his case and coat in the back of the car again, before he got into the driving seat. The traffic around them was moving off slowly, and the policeman who he had talked to, gave him a smile as he gestured for him to enter the stream of traffic. "Were you alright on your own?" he asked, as they crawled past a heap of metal on the side of the road. There were a couple of ambulances and a fire engine, as well as police cars, and she shot a glance at

him. "I was fine" she said, "but what happened? I take it, that those cars were the people who you called idiots, and said that they were an accident waiting to happen?"
"Yes, and they did have an accident. They managed to hit each other, but by good fortune, nobody else was involved. They're being taken to hospital now, and I'm afraid that their racing days are over, for a long while. If only other idiots could see the chaos they cause, perhaps they wouldn't be so keen as to get from A to B as soon as they could." He shook his head at the foolishness of people. "We should be able to stop for lunch fairly soon, I expect you're getting hungry? I know I am."
"I'm okay" she said quietly. "But you stop when you want to. The puppy's still asleep. He woke up once, barked twice and went back to sleep." Hayden smiled, and the journey continued.

By the time they reached Hayden's house that evening, she was tired. The car was very comfortable, and she hadn't done anything, which was perhaps the reason why she didn't get to sleep very easily that night. They had stopped several times to make sure that the puppy was okay, but she hadn't done much exercise, for the weather had still been very bad, and Hayden didn't want her to get too wet. The meal that Mrs. Bates had cooked, had been waiting for them, had been all that she had wanted, and she went to bed quite contented with life. Hayden had kissed her on the cheek again, that seemed to be his normal way of acknowledging her, and she knew she felt happy. The puppy had been given some food and drink, and tucked up in a large puppy crate in one of the warm rooms off the kitchen, and she knew she had nothing to worry about, for Hayden had told her that he would make sure a vet called in the next day or two, to look the puppy over and make sure it was healthy and give him its first vaccine. She had gone up to bed, had a long hot bath, and thoroughly relaxed, she had tried to sleep, but when she closed her eyes, she had seen again, the heap of twisted metal they had passed on the motorway after he had gone to give assistance. She hadn't been able to tell Hayden, but she had been scared out of her wits when he had gone to help deal with the accident, worrying about him, and wondering what would happen to her, if he had been hurt. She felt as though she had become a burden to him, even though he had told her he wanted to look after her. She decided that she would call Mr. Rickards and find out what was happening, as soon as she could, and on that thought, she finally slept.

Chapter Six

When she went down to breakfast the following morning, Hayden wasn't at the table, but she could see him in the garden, and went to the French windows to look out. He had the puppy with him, on a long lead, and from that distance, she could see that it had recovered its spirits, and was running to and fro, before coming back to stand by Hayden's legs. She opened the window, and he looked up and smiled as he saw her. “He's had a little walk, and he seems to be enjoying himself.” he said, “Come on Pup, let's get you back inside, and your mum can see how you're doing.” The puppy planted its feet for a while, and didn't want to accompany him, until it suddenly saw Debby, and bounced towards her, running as fast as its legs could carry it. She had taken a step onto the patio, and now she bent to gather the little animal into her arms. He licked her face, and wriggled in her arms, and she smiled at his antics. “We'll have to think of a name for him” she said. “Just look at him bouncing around all over the place.” She looked up at Hayden, and smiled, “perhaps your suggestion of calling him Bouncer was the right one.” The puppy had stopped moving in her arms for a moment, and now his ears pricked up. “Shall we call you Bouncer?” she asked him, and he nuzzled his nose into her neck, and she could feel his tongue licking her. Hayden was watching them, and now he smiled at the picture they made. “Bouncer it shall be then” he said. “I'll take him back to his pen for a minute while we have breakfast, then we can make a plan for teaching him his manners.” She agreed, and reluctantly handed the little dog over to him, and went back into the breakfast room, shutting the French doors behind her. She was sitting at the table, when he returned and they were helping themselves to breakfast, when the housekeeper came into the room, with a handful of letters in her hand, which she put on the table. "Postie's been" she said, "One for you Mrs. T." and went out of the room again. Hayden picked up the letters and sorted them out. "She's right, there is one for you" he glanced at the postmark, and smiled. "I bet it's from Mr. Rickards." She took it and opened it, pulled out the sheets of paper therein, and started to read it. He looked at her, for she had a frown on her face, and said "Trouble?" She nodded, and handed him the letter. He took it and read, and his smile disappeared. "How can your uncle insist that your father wanted him to have the business if he passed away?" he asked, and she shook her head. "Dad's will said that everything was to come to me, if you remember rightly? He left everything to me, apart from the bequest to charity, but now, my uncle is insisting he has a document signed in front of witnesses, saying that if anything happened to my father, the company was to go to him. Hayden, I don't believe this?"

"No, but look at the final paragraph. Rickards has written that he doesn't believe this is true, and will be demanding to see the documents, and will be having them examined by a graphologist. Don't worry Debby, it's just that odious man trying to stop you taking control of the business. I bet this is a delaying tactic, so he can syphon off the cash, to a different place, and then he'll tell you that there's no money available.

Rickards will stop that, if he can, in fact I think I'll phone him this morning, and we can have a discussion about what to do. But Debby, don't worry about anything. You're quite okay to live here with me for as long as you like. I've told you I'll look after you, and if Rickards can't do anything and get any money back from your uncle, well, I've got plenty, and you're quite welcome to have anything you want of mine."

"Thank you," she said quietly, "it's just that I owe you so much already, and I don't like being in debt to anybody."

"Deborah, you are my wife, and as such, you don't owe me anything at all. Don't you remember the words of the wedding service, for richer, for poorer, in sickness and in health? I meant what I said Debby, and as for being in debt, well, don't be silly. Now," he gathered up the papers on the table, and put them back in the envelope. "Finish your breakfast, I'll go and phone Rickards, and then we can go and sort out Bouncer." And he poured her more coffee, and offered more toast. She grinned, and obediently took more toast and poured another cup of coffee.

She had cleared the table of its used crockery, and carrying the tray, she went into the kitchen. "There's no need for you to do that Mrs. T.," the housekeeper said, but she was smiling and Debby didn't feel as if she were usurping the other woman's duties. Hayden had gone to his study, but now he emerged with a grin on his face. "Just as we thought. Mr. Rickards has already put an order in, to stop any money being moved from the company account to a different one, and has engaged a graphologist to examine the documents.

He's doing all he can for you. But let's go and get Bouncer, and we can think how we can train him." Reassured now, Deborah allowed herself to be led into the small room off the kitchen, where Bouncer was examining his pen. He looked up as they came in, and he came to the bars, and whined to get Deborah's attention. She opened the door of the cage and he bounded out, and went to her. She stroked his head, and he sat by her, allowing one ear to flop across his eye. She laughed as she looked at him, and Hayden thought how much happier she looked in the short time he had known her. They played with the little dog for a while, incorporating play into the training process, until he curled up in the corner of the cage, and Deborah shut the door behind her, as she left him alone. "He's lovely Hayden. Thank you so much for letting me have him." she said, and he put his arm around her shoulders and gave her a hug, as they left the room. "I've got some work to be getting on with" he said, "so perhaps you'd be able to find something else to get on with, before lunch." She nodded, and they went into the hall together, he to go to his study, and she went into the sitting room. She sat down by the fireplace, but although she had said she could do other things there wasn't much for her to do, and she knew she would feel bored, so she went back to the kitchen, to ask the housekeeper if there was anything she wanted. "I can go shopping If you want anything from the shops" she suggested, and the housekeeper shot her a glance. She recognised boredom when she saw it, and didn't want the younger girl to feel that way. "Okay Mrs. T., if you'd like to go to the shops, I wouldn't mind if you could get me a few items please", and sat down at the kitchen table. "I'll just write a list" she said, "while you go and get your coat on. It's cold outside you know." Deborah nodded, and went upstairs. While she was there, she made her bed, and tidied up the room, put a few items in the washing basket, picked up her coat and handbag, and went downstairs again. She didn't tell Hayden where she was going, but picked up the list from Mrs. Bates, and collecting a shopping bag, she went out of the front door. She walked slowly to the row of shops that were near the house, did the shopping that Mrs. Bates wanted, and at the end of the row, found a little shop that sold knitting and embroidery items, and went inside. The lady who ran it, smiled at her as she entered, "Can I help you my dear?" she asked, and Deborah looked around her. "I need to do something with my hands" she said. "Otherwise, I'll get bored, but I don't know what I can do." The lady smiled at her. "I know the feeling" she said. "That's why I started this place. It gives me the chance to meet lots of people, and I can spend my time knitting while I don't have customers. Can you knit my dear?"

"Well, I was taught by my mother, but it was a long time ago, and I can't remember how to start or finish, and I'm very slow at the bit in the middle." They laughed together, and the woman introduced herself. "I'm Elizabeth Little" she said. "Would you like to start some knitting? I don't mind teaching you, and you'd enjoy it I think."

"I'd love to," said Deborah. "I'm Deborah Parkes, and I live fairly locally. If you could teach me, I'd be very grateful." They discussed what Deborah would require and made arrangements as to when she could visit,

and have a lesson, before Deborah remembered she would have to get back to the house. She said her goodbyes, and made her way back to Hayden's house. He was standing waiting for her in the hallway, and looked angry. “Where on earth have you been?” he asked. “I thought you'd been kidnapped, or something.”
“I went shopping for Mrs. Bates” and she held out the bag, as evidence.
“Where else?” he queried. “When Mrs. Bates told me you'd gone to the shops I went down to meet you, and couldn't see sight nor sound of you.”
“I was in the knitting shop” she said quietly. “I'm sorry, I didn't know you'd follow me, but I was talking to the lady who owns it, and I forgot the time.”
“Did you buy anything?” he asked, but she shook her head, unwilling to tell him she was going to have lessons. He sighed, “Well, take that lot through to Mrs. Bates, and we can have lunch. We are going to take Bouncer to the vet this afternoon, and he can have his first vaccination. The first step to his new life with you.” She shrugged out of her coat, and he took it from her, and placed it on the chair in the hall, and she went through to the kitchen, where she handed over the shopping. “Sorry I took so long” she said quietly, “I was talking to the lady in the wool shop.”
“Oh, Elizabeth Little” said Mrs. Bates with a smile. “We're old friends. Are you going to make something?” Deborah nodded. “I want to try and make a sweater” she said, “but I can't remember how to start or finish off, so Mrs. Little is going to teach me.”
“She's a nice lady is Elizabeth,” said the housekeeper. “Now Mrs. T., lunch is ready if you'd like to go and sit

yourself down." Feeling as if she had been dismissed, Deborah went into the dining room, and she and Hayden were soon eating a delicious soup and hot rolls. "She's a good cook, isn't she?" Deborah asked. "Do you think she'd object if I did some cooking when she's not here?"

"Don't see why not" he said. "You are after all, her employer."

"No, I'm not" Deborah gasped, and Hayden smiled at the expression on her face. "You are, you know" he looked at her. "Technically I suppose I employ her, but you're married to me, so, you're her employer as well."

Deborah shook her head, and grinned. "I never thought of that" she said, then remembered that she had told Mrs. Little that she was Deborah Parkes, and hadn't given the woman her married name. "What's the matter now?" Hayden asked, for he had seen the expression on her face. "Nothing" she said hurriedly, "I forgot something, and I've just remembered it. No problem really." She went on spooning her soup, and Hayden looked sharply at her, and wondered exactly what she had been up to. He didn't think that her uncle would do something as underhand as kidnapping her, but the older man could easily make her life a misery, if he found out where she was living.

The afternoon trip to the vet, passed smoothly. Bouncer was given a full check-up, and although he was small, he was given a clean bill of health. "I presume you saw him with his mother?" the vet asked, and Hayden grinned. "She belongs to my parents, and he was the only one of the litter who hadn't been sold. Dad said he always seemed to be vicious and snapped

at anybody who came to view him, almost as though he was waiting for Debby. And I saw how he behaved when somebody else picked him up. When she first saw him, they fell in love with each other, and we decided to have him. He was the runt of the litter, which is another reason why he wasn't taken."
"I'm surprised he wasn't snapped up" the vet said, "Blue Merle's are quite rare, and he's going to be a beauty. Let's hope his ears stand up properly."
"I don't care if they don't" Deborah said firmly. "I think that one ear flopping downwards gives him an appealing look."
"You wouldn't be able to show him, if his ears don't stand up" the vet said, but she shook her head. "I don't intend to show him. He's my pet and my friend.", and she gave the puppy a big hug, and he licked her neck. Hayden grinned at the vet. "I think that's fairly definite then." he said. "If you can give him his first vaccinations, and microchip him, that will be fine. We'll bring him back for his next vaccines in a couple of weeks' time." Deborah couldn't watch as Bouncer was injected by the vet, but knew it was the best thing for him, to be protected against all the diseases he could potentially get. The vet handed her a bundle of leaflets. "There's a lot of advice in these, about feeding, socialising, going in a car, etc., so they might be a help for you. But I think your husband knows quite a bit about puppy care, and he'll be able to help you" he said. Deborah thanked him, and picked up Bouncer, to give him another hug. "It's very obvious who he has taken to, as his new mum" said the vet as he watched her put the puppy back in his travelling crate. "It was like that from the first moment" said

Hayden softly, and the two men exchanged grins.

"Do you want to go out for the day tomorrow?" Hayden asked, when they got home, but she shook her head. "I'll stay at home, and I can continue teaching Bouncer his first manners" she said, and grinned. "Well, remember, he'll spend quite a bit of time asleep" he said, and she nodded. "I might go shopping again, while he's sleeping" she replied, as she went upstairs to take her coat off. Hayden frowned, as he watched her go, and wondered what she wanted to buy. He wasn't to know she was eager to go through her mother's sewing box, which was one of the few items she had retrieved, when her uncle had cleared the house, find out exactly what was in it and then purchase the wool to start her jumper. When she came downstairs later on, Hayden had moved the puppy crate into the lounge, and Bouncer was still asleep in it. She smiled at Hayden, as she watched the puppy sleep, and sat near him, stroking his head. "As you don't want to go out for the day, do you want to go out to dinner tomorrow night?" Hayden asked, and she nodded. "That would be nice, thank you."
"I'll be starting work soon, so there won't be too much opportunity after that" he said, and she nodded. "Where do you want to go to?" he asked, but she didn't know. "You choose" she said. "I don't know many places." she said, and smiled at her husband. Hayden looked at her, and saw the difference in her since he had first met her. She had put on weight, and looked much healthier than she had done, her hair was loose, but caught back with a ribbon, so the scar didn't show as much, and of course, the new clothes did help

a lot. He had known she would repay for dressing, but hadn't realised how much. "Wear something pretty" he said. "That long blue dress you bought is nice. Do you want to go dancing afterwards?" Her eyes lit up, and she nodded. "Please" she said. When Mrs. Bates bought a tray of tea in, Hayden told her they would be out for dinner the following evening, and the housekeeper nodded. "You'll enjoy that" she said. "I'll keep an eye on the little one." and she looked at Bouncer. "I like dogs and when my husband was alive, we often had young ones. If you don't mind me feeding him, that is?" and she looked earnestly at Deborah. "Thank you for the offer Mrs. Bates. I don't mind at all. I was a bit worried about going out and leaving him on his own."

"Don't you fret Mrs. T., I'll keep an eye on him. Now, your tea's there, if you'd like to pour it out." and she turned and went out the room. "There you are," Hayden said. "you've got a willing person to keep an eye on him, when you need to go out. When I start work again, I'll try and be home in the evenings, but there will be times when I can't make it, you know that don't you?" Deborah nodded, and wondered how often he would be out. She poured the tea, and handed him a plate with the slice of cake he asked for, and she wondered what she would do in the evenings, when Hayden wasn't there, then remembered that she would have her knitting to get on with. Hayden was watching her face, and knew when she'd thought of something. "Hayden," she said "you remember when Mrs. McKendrick said about a little one helping? Do you think she might have meant Bouncer? I'd only just seen him for the first time when we met her."

"I remember, and I did wonder about that. Lots of people have called him the little one – Mrs. Bates, the lady in the pub we stopped at, and the vet as well. Maybe she did mean him, but hopefully we won't find out for quite a while. By then, you'll be more at home here, and he'll spend more time awake, and you'll be able to take him to meet other dogs, and he can go for walks outside the garden. He'll soon grow and he won't be a little one for long." Deborah smiled at him. "Hope so" she replied, and dropped the subject. "Do you want more tea?" she asked, and he passed his cup to be refilled. They spent the evening together, talking occasionally, and listening to music, something she hadn't been able to do for a while, and by the time she went to bed, she felt happier than she had done for a long time.

The days passed, and when she looked back afterwards, she realised she was happy. Bouncer was doing very well, and even in the few days she had had him, she realised he was learning a lot, and growing well. Hayden had taken her out to dinner as he had promised, and they had gone dancing afterwards. Their steps matched well, and she hadn't felt awkward with him at all. He had kissed her gently at the end of the evening, and she had gone to bed, feeling extremely happy and content with life. She knew she had done the right thing in marrying him, it was only when she thought about an annulment that she began to worry, but she was realistic enough to know this wouldn't happen for a while. He had taken her shopping for clothes again, and realised what good taste he had. She knew he was going to be starting work at the hospital very soon, and when Sunday arrived, and they'd come back from church, she knew this was their last full day together. He had taken her for a walk in one of the local parks, and he'd held her hand, and it was when she was changing for dinner that evening, she knew that she was going to miss him, and would be glad when he returned from the hospital every day.

When she went down to breakfast the next day, Hayden had left the house already, and she felt a bit lonely, but decided she had to keep herself busy. The decision made, she saw to Bouncer's needs, asked Mrs. Bates if she wanted anything done, and when her offer of help was refused, decided to go and see Mrs. Little. The woman greeted her with a smile, and after a short discussion about what she wanted to make, showed her a selection of sweaters. After some deliberation, Deborah decided on one, and with a good heart, she started her first lesson. As the lesson proceeded, some of her mother's teachings came back to her, and by the time, lunchtime came around, she had remembered a lot, and she packed up the work, and started back to the house. There was a very cold wind blowing, and she kept her head down, but as she approached the front door, she saw a person moving near it, and instinctively drew into the shelter between two of the houses in the road. The man looked up at Hayden's house, and she gasped, for this was her cousin Dudley. She had no wish to meet him, and waited until he moved off, and walked away. Deborah waited until he had gone round the corner, then ran to the house, and let herself in, shutting the door firmly behind her. She went down to the kitchen, and Mrs. Bates looked up as she entered. She was wild eyed, and the housekeeper eyed her with concern. "Why Mrs. T., what's the problem?" she asked. Deborah sat at the kitchen table. "Did anybody knock at the door?" she asked, and was slightly reassured by the negative response. "No, there's been no visitors at all." was the reply. "Why do you ask?"

"Because I've just seen my cousin hanging around outside, and I've got no desire to meet him at all." she said. "If he ever asks for me, can you tell him I'm not here, please Mrs. Bates?" She was shivering, and the housekeeper looked concerned at her reaction. "Of course I will" she said. "Don't you fret Mrs. T., I won't let anything happen to you. The master, he asked me to make sure that you're safe, and I'll do my level best. Now, you just go and take that coat off, and I'll serve your lunch. Why don't you phone the master this afternoon and tell him you've seen the cousin, and ask his advice?

"No, I can't do that" she said, "he's only just started this new job, and I don't want to disturb him. I'll tell him this evening, and see what he says. But I've had an idea" she smiled tremulously at the woman, "I might phone my solicitor, and see what he suggests."

"That's a good idea Mrs. T. Now, just go and sit down and have some lunch." Deborah did as she had been instructed, and that afternoon, feeling slightly better for the meal, she phoned Mr. Rickards. "Well, my dear, I can't do anything to stop him seeing you" he said. "I think I'll tell your husband about it though, and see if he can suggest anything. Did this Dudley ever injure you in any way?"

“Not physically.” she said, “He would let his father do that, but he would hold me down, while his father hit me, and he would do things like turn up when we were just about to start eating, and take my dinner away and eat it himself. He's his father's solicitor as well, so I think he's the one who is encouraging him to take control of everything. I know it’s got to be him, who forged my signature on those papers, and I wouldn't put it past him to have forged the paper from my father, giving control to my uncle, if dad died. Oh Mr. Rickards, I wish dad hadn't died, everything seems to have gone wrong since then.”

“Yes, well, we're working on that” he said, “I was going to phone you and ask if you'd got a sample of your father's handwriting? That would help the graphologist we've got looking at that paper.”

“I've got a couple of birthday cards that dad sent me when I was younger” she said, “but I would like them back. I don't have much of dad's handwriting anyway, and those cards are precious.”

“Of course you'd get them back my dear. If I might visit you tomorrow, I can collect them, if that would be convenient?”

“Of course, it would be. What time would you like to come? You could stay for lunch if you wanted to.”

“That's very kind of you to offer my dear, but I don't think so. If I come to the house about mid-morning, will you have the cards ready for me?” She agreed, and they said their goodbyes. When she had put the phone down, she went upstairs to find the cards and put them in an envelope ready for the solicitor, and sat down to think. She hadn't reached any conclusions, when she heard Bouncer barking, and smiled as she thought of looking after the puppy, and went to see how he was. He wanted to play, and she put her coat on again, and took him out to the garden, where the little puppy bounced around the garden, obviously enjoying his new freedom. When he was tired, she took him indoors, and he went to sleep in front of the fire, and she sat with him, enjoying his company, and drifted off to sleep with his head on her lap.

She awoke to hear the front door knocker being beaten ferociously, and Bouncer was standing by the door, alternately growling or barking loudly. She got to her feet and glanced out the window, and saw Dudley standing on the doorstep, and shrank back into the shadows. She heard Mrs. Bates go and answer the door, heard the rumble of her cousin's voice, Mrs. Bates replying, "No sorry, she doesn't live here" and then her cousin shouted again, "well, just tell her she's not going to get a penny, and we'll see her rot in hell before she does", before he walked away. Bouncer was still barking, and she heard the front door shut, and opened the lounge door. Bouncer immediately charged to the front door, still barking loudly, and Deborah grabbed him, and held him close. The housekeeper took her hand in his, and Deborah could see that the woman was white, and shaking. "Let's go down to the kitchen, and we can stay there" she said. "I'll make us both a cup of tea, and then I'm phoning the solicitor again." She took Mrs. Bates down to the kitchen, put Bouncer in his pen, and made them both a cup of tea. "I'm sorry you had to put up with that" she said. "That was my cousin Dudley. He's an obnoxious man, just like his father, and they obviously think they can intimidate me, and you." She sighed. "I think I might wait for Hayden to come home and tell him what happened, and he can tell me what to do. But wasn't Bouncer good? He obviously thinks that I needed protection from that horrible man." The housekeeper had regained some of her colour now, and she was able to smile with Deborah. "He obviously didn't believe me when I said you didn't live here" she said and Deborah nodded. "I wonder if I might do better to go right away from here, somewhere where they won't be able to find me, and try and intimidate me again?" she said, but the housekeeper shook her head. "No, my dear. Your husband will be home soon, and he'll tell you what to do. Besides, you wouldn't want to leave Bouncer now, would you? And he couldn't go with you. He's got to have the rest of his inoculations before he can go outside, and you're doing so well with him. Look at him, he's worn himself out, barking like that." Deborah looked over to the pen, and saw that Bouncer was asleep again, his paw on the teddy bear that Hayden had bought with him when he left his litter mates. "I wish he was a bit older, so he could be a proper guard dog" she said, "then he could have bitten Dudley." The housekeeper laughed, and the two women sat together to wait for Hayden's return.

It was earlier than Deborah had expected, when Hayden returned, to find both ladies sitting in the kitchen, nursing mugs of tea. He entered the room, and Bouncer woke, sat up and barked at him. "That's a nice welcome" he laughed, then saw the way the two ladies didn't respond to his laughter. "What's the problem?" he said, his expression changing, and bent

his head to kiss Deborah on the cheek. “Dudley turned up” she said. “He banged on the door, didn't listen when Mrs. Bates told him I didn't live here, just yelled, that I wasn't going to get a penny, and they'd see me rot in hell before I did. How did they find out that you live here? It really scared me, I can tell you, but when I was walking back from the shop this morning, I saw him and he was hanging around outside. I waited until he'd walked away before I could get back here, and feel safe behind the front door. But I just don't feel safe anymore. Even Bouncer didn't like him, he was barking all the time that Dudley was at the front door. He was really rude to Mrs Bates as well.”
“Did you tell anybody? Mr. Rickards or the police?” he asked, and she shook her head. “Mr. Rickards phoned this morning and said he's dealing with things, and wants some samples of my father's handwriting, and he's coming tomorrow morning to collect them.” Hayden smiled grimly. “They're getting worried, I think.” he said “Don't fret Debby, I'm going to phone the police now, and ask them to keep an eye on the house. I don't think Dudley will be back again, - he's delivered the message, and now they're going to wait until the lawyers decide what to do.” He kissed her cheek again, and smiled at Mrs. Bates. “Don't worry, you'll be safe behind the doors of this house, and if necessary, I'll arrange for somebody to keep an eye on it, while I'm at the hospital. So, I don't suppose you felt like getting dinner tonight, did you? I'll take you both out for a meal.” and despite all Mrs. Bates' protestations, that is what he did.

Chapter Seven

Winter was well on its way, and Deborah wrapped up warmly to take Bouncer for a walk in the park. It had been five weeks since Dudley had appeared on the doorstep, but there had been no sign of him since then. Bouncer had had his second vaccinations, and the vet had told her that she could take him for a short walk in the park, where he might meet other dogs. He seemed to like going into the big outdoors, but tired quickly, so she only took him for short walks. Whenever he was free, which was usually at weekends, Hayden would accompany them, and she enjoyed being in his company. The walk was swiftly accomplished, for Bouncer didn't appear to like the cold wind that seemed to blow all the time, and was pleased to get back to the house, and his pen in the warm room off the kitchen. He was responding well to training, would come when called, if only in the garden, and knew his name. He was eating well and putting on weight and Deborah couldn't believe how much he had grown since they had bought him home. She opened the front door, and led the excited puppy back to his crate, where he settled down for a refreshing sleep. Mrs. Bates smiled as she looked at him. “I can't imagine life without him now” she said. “I must admit when Mr. Hayden phoned and told me we were going to have a puppy in the house, I was a bit apprehensive, but he's such a little darling.” She picked up a handful of letters from the kitchen table. “I was just going to take these into the sitting room for you. Postman's getting later each day, what with increased

post because Christmas is just around the corner."
"Do you want me to do anything to get a room ready for Mr. and Mrs. Tomlinson when they come?" she asked, but the housekeeper shook her head. "No thanks," she said. "it's all ready for them." Deborah was a bit apprehensive about her parents-in-law visiting them, especially, as one of Hayden's sisters would be coming as well, ostensibly to go shopping with her mother, but Deborah knew there had been a lot of speculation among her sisters-in-law, as to what she was like. "I've put them in their usual room, and I've made the room next to it ready for Miss Katrina. I understand she's not bringing her husband with her?" Deborah smiled at the memory of the conversation she had had with her sister-in-law, "No, she reckoned it would be easier if I were to meet her on her own first of all. When I've met just one of the sisters, we can all go to his parents' house and everybody else will come and we can meet there. It will be nice to see Hayden's parents again though. They were really kind to me when I visited them."
"Well, I'll bring you in a cup of coffee and you can drink that, while you read your post." Mrs. Bates said, and taking that as a strong hint that the housekeeper wanted her out of the kitchen, Deborah went. The housekeeper was right – there was a great deal of post, and she sorted it out, putting those for Hayden on one side, and opening the others. There were quite a few Christmas cards from people she had never even heard of, let alone met, and she wondered who they were, but one of the envelopes was typewritten, and she opened it, and pulled out a gilt-edged card. They were invited to the Hospital Ball, to be held in the Ballroom

of the Hospital the following week. She put it to one side, knowing that her parents-in-law would be here while the Ball was taking place, and knew that it wasn't likely that she would be able to attend. When Hayden came in that evening, a lot later than usual, he looked tired, and she knew instinctively that he wouldn't want to bother about invitations. They had eaten their meal, and were sitting quietly in the sitting room, when he opened the letters, she had put to one side, then picked up the envelope containing the invitation. "Oh, they finally sent them out" he said with a smile, "I was wondering when I was going to get my invitation."

"We won't be able to go" Deborah said quietly, "your parents and sister will be visiting, and we can't go out in the evening and leave them to themselves."

"We will be going" he said firmly, "Mum, Dad and Katrina will probably go and visit grandmother then, so we'll be able to attend. You'll have to go and buy a grand dress. If you ask her nicely, mum will probably go with you, and of course, Katrina will be here, and she adores shopping. You won't have any problem finding somebody to help you choose." he grinned at her, and she smiled back. He was so good to her, buying her things, and she determined that she would pay him back every penny when she was able to. "Okay," she said. "I think I'll go to town and see what I can find."

"And remember, it's got to be a grand dress" he said. "Everybody will expect to..." he stopped, then "all eyes will be upon you, as I'm the newest surgeon, they will want to know who I've married."

"Wouldn't it be easier if I don't meet all your friends?" she said, "after all, if, I mean, when we part, then you'll have to explain everything, and it would probably be easier if they hadn't met me, and known who I was."

"Let's cross that bridge when we come to it," he said quietly, and she nodded. "Okay" she agreed, and lapsed into silence, wondering why she suddenly felt so sad. "What have you been doing today?" Hayden asked her, and she shrugged "Just the normal things, taking Bouncer for a couple of short walks, I don't think he likes the cold wind, because he always wants to get back into the warm as soon as he can, I did some knitting, and I went and got a few items for Mrs. Bates, this morning." He was looking intently at her, and as she was looking down at her hands, she didn't see the look he was giving her. "Debby, are you happy?" he asked and she looked up at him. "Yes, oh yes" she said. "You can't believe how it feels to be free of my aunt and uncle, able to eat all I want, being able to buy all my lovely new clothes, and I've got Bouncer as well. Of course I'm happy." He was smiling at her, but the smile didn't seem to reach his eyes. "Good" he said, "I'm glad everything's okay." She didn't know what to say, but instead asked, "What about you, what have you being doing today?"

"Oh, I had a couple of operations to do, which is why I'm a bit late, and a big round this morning. Why do you ask?"

"Because you look tired." she answered honestly. "I know you got called out a couple of nights ago, and you were in the hospital most of the night, but you didn't look tired then, but today, you do. Are you alright?"

"Don't fret about me" he said quietly, as he came to stand beside her, and took her hand in his. "I'm fine.

Just got a few tricky patients on the wards. It will calm down fairly soon I expect." He bent and kissed her gently on the lips. "Thank you, Deborah," he said, then he turned away, picked up one of the letters he had placed on the table by the side of him, and started to read it. Deborah looked at him, and suddenly knew that she didn't want the marriage to end. She knew that she wanted to stay with him, for their marriage to be a real one, and knew that she loved him. She gasped, and he looked at her. "Everything okay?" he asked and she nodded. "I think I'll have an early night" she said. "I'll go and have a bath, and then go to bed. Do you reckon you'll be home for dinner tomorrow?"

"I hope so" he said. "I'll let you know if I'm going to be late." he stood up as she got to her feet. "Goodnight Debby" he said, and bent his head to kiss her on the cheek. "Sleep well." and she left the room.

When she reached her bedroom, she sat staring into the middle distance. Knowing that she was in love with him, was a shock, and she didn't know how to cope with it. She didn't know how long she sat there but eventually got up and went into the bathroom, to run herself a long hot bath. She lay in it for a while, trying not to think about a future without Hayden, and sobbing now, she got out, wrapped herself in a bathrobe, and went back into the bedroom, where she donned her nightdress, and got into bed. She turned the light out, and lay back against the pillows, and eventually drifted into sleep. She woke in the early hours, her face wet with tears, and knew she was going to have to avoid seeing Hayden in the morning, for he would see that she had been crying, and didn't know how to explain her red eyes and nose. She had hoped that Hayden would have gone by the time she went downstairs that morning, but he was sitting at the table, drinking coffee. He looked closely at her as she came into the room, and frowned. "Are you alright?" he asked and she nodded. "I'm fine" she said, "just didn't sleep too well."

"I can see that" he said. "Why not have a nice relaxing day here, and I'll see you this evening."

"I always have relaxing days" she said, "I never do anything stressful." She resented the fact that he thought she had days when she had to worry. "Well, just take Bouncer for a couple of walks, and I'll see you tonight." he put his cup down, kissed her on the cheek, and left the room. She stared after him, wondering what he would do if she threw her arms around him and told him of her love for him, and knew it would never happen. Mrs. Bates came in, with Bouncer bounding around her, and she bent and patted the puppy. "I'll take him for a walk in a bit" Deborah said, and the housekeeper took a good look at her face. "What's the problem Mrs. T.?" she asked. "You don't look very happy at the moment. Who's upset you?"

"Nobody" Deborah said "I just didn't sleep very well" she said, "I'll take Bouncer out for a walk, and that will relax me. If I walk far enough, I'll wear myself out, and hopefully I'll be able to sleep properly tonight."

"Well, you can't take Bouncer for a very long walk. He wouldn't be able to cope with it."

"Don't worry Mrs. Bates, I'll bring him back before I go out again. I don't think I'll be in to lunch, so don't worry about getting anything for me."

"You need something to eat" she was told. "Now, just sit there, and I'll bring you in some toast and some more coffee."
"I don't want any toast" she said stubbornly, "And I don't really want any coffee thank you."
"Mrs. T., you must eat something. You were thin enough when you first moved in here. If you don't eat, you'll lose all the weight you've put on, and believe me, it won't suit you."
Deborah turned away from the woman. "I promise I'll eat something tonight, but just at the moment, I'm not hungry if you don't mind." she said quietly, and the housekeeper took a long look at her. "I'll come and get his harness, and take Bouncer out" Deborah said quietly. "I'll just go and get my coat." and she left the room and shut the door. Bouncer started to bark, but the housekeeper who was clearing the table, hushed him. "Your mum will be back in a minute" she said. "Then she'll take you for a walk. You look after her, 'cos she's not happy" she told the dog, and he obediently sat down in front of the door. Deborah returned carrying her coat, and Bouncer's harness. "See you later" she said, and left the house, with the dog prancing around her legs.

She returned with Bouncer about 30 minutes later, and took him into his pen. "I'll be back soon" she said, "I'll go for a long walk and think about things."
"What have you got to think about?" asked the housekeeper, and was shocked when Deborah said shortly, "My future" before she headed out again. Deborah walked for miles around the streets where the house was situated, even going past her old house at

one point, until she realised where she was and hurried away, walking until she was tired, not caring that she hadn't eaten or drunk anything, and she was thinking about going back to the house, when she went past the knitting shop. Mrs. Little saw her as she went past and came to the door. "Hello Miss Parkes" she said, and Deborah realised she'd never told the woman her married name. "Hello, Mrs. Little" she said. "How's things?"

"Oh, I'm doing alright" she replied. "But I haven't seen you for a long time. How are you keeping?"

"I'm just a bit worried" she said, "I found out something yesterday, and its worried me ever since I discovered it."

"What's that then my dear?" queried the older woman. "Or don't you feel that you could tell me?"

"It's a bit personal" she said, but she wanted to talk to somebody – somebody who wasn't connected with the family. "Well, come in and have a drink, and you can tell me, if you want to. I'm not going to push you, but if you want to talk, you can." and she opened the door wide, and Deborah went into the shop. "Come through to the back" she said, as she turned the sign on the door to read closed, and she led the way through to the room behind the shop. There she put the kettle on, and bade Deborah to sit down, while she put out cups and saucers. When the drink was ready, she sat down opposite Deborah, and smiled at her. "So, what's the problem?" she asked. "You don't look very happy today, and I'm hoping that it's nothing to do with your uncle."

"How did you know about my uncle?" Deborah asked, and the other woman laughed. "I'm sorry dear, the answer is your Mrs. Bates of course. Emma Bates and I have been friends for a long time, and she's told me a lot about you and your family. And of course, I knew your father as well. He advised me on how to turn this house into a shop. He and I became good friends, but that was a long time ago, and I think you need a friend now."

"Yes, Dad's been dead now for about five years" she said. "When he died, he left me everything, but my uncle and aunt basically stole it from me." She shrugged. "My uncle made me act as his slave, didn't feed me as well as he should have done, and although I wanted to rebel, he would hit me if I tried anything, so I didn't think I could escape. That is, until Hayden came to see him to get some quotes for work to be done on his grandmother's house, and realised that there was a problem. He married me to get me away from my uncle and aunt, and I'm staying in his house until my solicitor can get something sorted out." She told the woman everything about the way she had ended up in hospital after her uncle's attack on her, and Hayden's unconventional proposal. She talked herself to a standstill, and the woman looked at her. "And what did you discover yesterday?" she asked, "Did you realise you were in love with him?"

Deborah sat up straight. "How did you know that, or was it a lucky guess?" she said, and swallowed the tears that were crowding her throat, as she realised, she was going to cry if she wasn't careful. "The way you talk about him" was the answer. "And what about him? Doesn't he have any feelings for you at all?"

"I don't know" Deborah said, having thought about that since the night before, "he's been incredibly generous to me, giving me clothes and things, and of course, he gave me Bouncer, but I don't know if he has any feelings for me. He's kissed me a few times, and I liked it when he did it, but I don't think I know anything at all. But last night, we were talking, and I told him it was a shame that he was going to introduce me to his friends at the Hospital Ball, because when we part, then he's going to have to explain to everybody why I've gone, and I don't want him to suffer in the future."

"Debby my dear" Mrs. Little said, "don't worry about this. I'm sure he's got some feelings for you, and he'll continue to look after you. It's obvious he likes you, because I don't think he would have asked you to marry him, unless he felt something for you. Just let things go on as they are" she advised. "Carry on, until your solicitor can make sure that you will be able to support yourself if anything happened, and then you can make a decision, and by then, you might have some idea of how Hayden feels about you." she smiled, "I can assure you my dear, I will never ever tell anybody what you have told me. But you can always come and talk to me, if you feel the need. Your father and I got on so well, and he helped me so much, and I would like to think I could help his daughter. And, of course, I will always be pleased to see you again." Debby nodded and the other woman changed the subject. "Now, how is your knitting getting on? Have you managed the shaping on the neck yet?"

"I'm just starting to do it" she said, "I think it's alright, but if I bring it in, could you have a look at it, and see if it's okay?"

"Of course I can my dear. Bring it in and I'll have a look at it, and we can share a cup of tea as well. You could

always bring Bouncer in as well, and I can see how he's grown. I've seen him when you've walked him past the shop, and he's a lovely little dog." She grinned at Deborah. "I hear he doesn't like your cousin? was barking fit to burst when he went to the house"
"Yes," Deborah agreed "If he was bigger and had his adult teeth, I think I would have let him have a go at Dudley. I'd love to see him sink his teeth into that man. I really don't like him at all. In fact, I hate him. He's an evil and obnoxious man, and his father is even worse!"
"Don't hold back" the woman smiled "but Emma Bates doesn't like him either." Mrs. Little nodded her head, and she and Deborah laughed together. She stayed for a little longer, then feeling better since she had told Mrs. Little how she felt, she said her farewells, and went back to the house, and Bouncer's ecstatic greeting. "Do you feel better now?" Mrs. Bates asked, when Deborah went into the kitchen, and she nodded. "I talked to Mrs. Little, and she's made me see sense, and I feel a bit better about things."
"Good" said the housekeeper. "Now, how about some tea? I bet you could eat something now, as you've not had anything all day?"
Deborah agreed, and went up the stairs to take her coat off, before she went into the sitting room. Bouncer went with her, and sat by her side. She stroked him, his unconditional love, soothing her frayed senses. "Oh Bouncer," she murmured, "What are we going to do? We're going to have to make some decisions about the future. Would you be very unhappy, if I left you here with your dad, if I left him? Or would you want to come and live with me?" Bouncer licked her face and she laughed. "I don't think

you're going to give me an answer, are you?" she said. The housekeeper opened the door and bought in a tray of tea and cakes, and the puppy sat up straight, looking longingly at the plate of food. "You're not having any of the cake" she laughed at him. "You can have your own food, but none of mine."

"You've got to be strict with him" said Mrs. Bates, and Deborah agreed. "I hope I am strict, but not too much" she said. "I've been reading all the books the vet gave me, and I think I'm doing everything right with his diet."

"You're doing well." she was told, "as long as he doesn't start to beg, because you can bet your bottom dollar that people will say, 'oh what a cute little doggy, let's give him some of this cake' and he'll get fat, and become ill."

"I don't think too many people will be visiting me" she said. "I can't really envisage my aunt or uncle visiting for tea, can you?"

"No, and if they turned up, then I think Bouncer might decide to eat them, instead of the other way round." Deborah laughed at the picture that conjured up, and was still laughing when the housekeeper left and Hayden walked in. "Just in time for tea" he said, as he kissed Deborah on the cheek. "Hello you, and hello Bouncer. Do you feel better now?" he asked, giving her a good look, and she nodded. "I went for a long walk, and thought about things, and then had a chat with a friend, and I feel a lot better now."

"Good" he said. "I managed to finish work early, so I thought I'd come home and take you out for dinner. Mum and Dad will be arriving tomorrow, so we won't have much time to ourselves, once they're here. And

Katrina is coming on the day afterwards. It will be nice to see her again, because I haven't seen her for a long while. It's a pity her husband can't come with her, but at least we'll be able to catch up again, and of course Mum and Dad will love to see her again." He smiled at her again. "Let's have something to drink, and then we can decide where to go out."

"Why ask me?" she said, "I've told you, I have no idea of any restaurants around this area. It's been years since Mum and Dad took me for a meal, and when Dad was alive, we didn't go to good restaurants, because I was too young." He smiled, and took her hand. "I'm sorry, I forgot. What about the place I took you to before I started work. Would you like to go back there again, and we can go dancing afterwards?" She nodded. "That sounds very nice" she said, "I've got a new dress, I haven't worn yet, so it can have an outing tonight." He smiled at her again, and she handed him his cup of tea, and offered a slice of the cake that Mrs. Bates had made. Bouncer was sitting at his feet, looking starved, and Deborah gave the puppy a stern glance. "Don't give him anything" she said. "I've just had a conversation with Mrs. Bates about feeding him things he shouldn't have. I don't want him to get fat."

"He won't get fat, but I won't let him have any treats he shouldn't have." They finished eating their tea, and Hayden reached down and stroked Bouncer's ears, and the puppy rubbed his head. "That ear still isn't standing up" he said, "I have doubts that it will actually ever stand up properly. Of course, it might, but if it doesn't will you be upset?"

"No," she replied, "It gives him character, I think. And it makes him look very appealing. He hasn't had a very long walk today. I walked him this morning, bought him home, and I don't think he's been out again. I didn't get in until about thirty minutes ago."

"Do you feel better?" he asked again, and she nodded. "I had to think something out, and I didn't come to any conclusions but I do feel better."

"Good" he said, and kissed her on the cheek. "Did you hear anything from Mr. Rickards?" he asked, but she shook her head. "I haven't even opened any post today. I went out straight after breakfast, and as I said, I didn't get in until later."

"Let's go and see if anybody has written to us then?" he said, and led the way to the study, making sure that Bouncer came with them. "If we leave him in here, he'll eat everything in sight" he said with a laugh, and led the way to his study. He sorted out the post, and handed her a couple of envelopes. She opened the first one, read it and handed it to Hayden. "How do they know that we'll be going to the Ball?" she asked. "We only got the invitation yesterday", for the letter was from one of the hospital governors' wives, inviting them to make up a party at the Ball. He laughed. "They will have invited all of the other surgical consultants as well" he said. "We aren't being singled out for special attention." She smiled, and then the smile faded as she looked at the other envelope. "It's from Mr. Rickards" she said quietly, and he took her hand in his. "We'll open it together" he said, "then if its bad news, you'll have somebody who can give you some advice if you need it." and he handed her the letter opener. The letter from the solicitor, was just keeping her up to date with what had happened so far. He had passed all the information to the lawyers who were assisting him, and all the information would be assessed, and then action would be taken using the information. Mr. Rickards hoped that they would soon be able to start retrieving some of Deborah's father's assets which could be passed on to Deborah. She took a deep breath as she read it, and Hayden took her hand. "Don't fret Debby" he said. "Things are starting to look up now, and you should soon be getting some of your father's assets. Hopefully, the company will be reverting to you very soon." Deborah nodded. "I don't know if I want to run a building company" she said. "I just don't want them to get all the benefit from it. But I would like to see them out of the house" she continued. "After all, that was my home from the time I was a child, and they just threw out all of my possessions, along with most of my dad's when they moved in. I think my father would have had something to say to them, had he known what they were going to do. I don't think he realised how greedy they were, otherwise he wouldn't have made Uncle Arthur the executor of his will."

"I think I agree with you" he said. "They obviously thought you would roll over and let them have everything and wouldn't disagree with them."

"Thank you" she said, and leaned forward to kiss him on the cheek. He turned his head, and their lips met, and her eyes widened. He broke the kiss, and smiled at her. "My reward" he said, and she smiled back at him. "I'll go and tell Mrs. Bates, we're going to go out, and then go and get changed" she said and went out into the hallway. Hayden looked after her as she went, and smiled as she went. He wanted her to have what she deserved, and he hoped he would be able to help her get it. He finished opening the post, before taking Bouncer for a short walk, before putting him back in his pen. The puppy was obviously tired, and curled up around the teddy bear that had been his friend since he had left his litter mates, and as it had their scent on it, he was not lonely.

When she came downstairs, she found Hayden waiting for her, and as she reached the bottom of the staircase, he whistled with admiration. Her dress was a pale pink, with long sleeves and a long skirt. It had a high neck, with a pleated bodice, and fitted her very well. She curtsied and he laughed. “Very nice” he said, and held out her coat. She pushed her arms into the sleeves, picked up her handbag, and Hayden escorted her out to the car. “I do like this car” she said. “It makes me feel very luxurious to be driven around in it.”
“Do you want to learn to drive it?” Hayden asked, and she shook her head. “No way” she said. “It's much too big for me, but I think I'd like to learn to drive something smaller, if possible.”
“Okay” he said, “I'll arrange for you to have lessons if you would like.” She smiled widely at him, as he shut the door behind her. “Oh, yes please” she said, “I'd like that.”
“I'll make some phone calls” he promised, and turned the engine on.

They reached the restaurant where they were to dine, and her coat was taken from her by the waiter. She chose her meal from the menu, and they danced together while they waited for the first course. They were taken into the restaurant by the waiter when it was ready, and after they'd finished their first course, they danced again. They dined together in harmony, and danced between courses. She loved being held in his arms, as he danced her around the floor. "At the hospital Ball" she began, "are there waltzes and foxtrots as well as modern stuff?" He shot a glance at her, and smiled. "Yes," he answered. "The first part will be the old-fashioned bits, then when all the bigwigs have gone, the nurses and doctors let themselves go, and dance until dawn."

"And what time do you normally leave" she asked, and he shot a glance at her head that was resting against his shoulder. "I have no idea" he said. "Don't forget, I only started at the hospital, just after I first met you."

"I thought you'd been there before" she said, but he shook his head. "I was at St. Chads in London when I was a student and got my first job there, when I'd qualified" he said. "After that, I went to Queens in Nottingham, then onto St. Davids in Edinburgh where I was a senior registrar and got my first consultant job, and where I did some further training. I applied for the job at Pearsons when it was advertised about four months ago. We've never really talked about my job, have we? Aren't you curious about what I do? Or are you not interested"

"I am interested" she said, "I didn't think you wanted to talk about it."

"I love talking about my job" he said. "Let's sit down, and I'll tell you about it." And they spent a while, just talking about what type of surgery he did. "I would have liked to think about being a nurse" she said, "and if Dad hadn't died, then I might have thought about applying to start training after I'd been to university.

But Uncle Arthur and Aunt Claudia put an end to that."
"We wouldn't have met unless you were on a ward that I had patients on" he said softly, and she nodded.
"I think I got the better part of the deal after all" she said, and they smiled at each other.
"I'll teach you about my work" he promised as they drove home again, and she knew she would be happy to have him do so.

Chapter Eight

Hayden's parents arrived in the afternoon of the following day, and as Hayden wasn't able to be at home at that time, Deborah was ready at the door ready to welcome them. Bouncer had been shut up in his pen, for she didn't want to run the risk of him running out of the garden. As the car drew up, and Eleanor got out, she came forward, and enfolded her mother-in-law in her arms. "Hello" she said simply, and was hugged in her turn. David gave her a big hug, and looked hard at her. "You look good" he said. "You've put on a bit more weight, and it suits you."

"You don't mean I'm getting fat?" she asked with horror, and both Eleanor and David laughed. "No, my dear" David said, "just that you're getting to be a lovely shape."

"Thank you," Deborah said. "Shall we go in? it's a bit cold out here" and she led the way inside. "Hayden didn't know exactly when you would be arriving" she said, "so he went into the hospital, and he's hoping to be able to get home a bit sooner than usual." and she escorted her guests into the lounge. "So, how's Bouncer?" she was asked, and she grinned. "Getting bigger and naughtier by the day" she said. "He'll know you're here, so I'll go and get him, and organise some tea for you both." At that moment, the door opened, and Mrs. Bates and Bouncer came in, the puppy yelping with delight, as he recognised more people to play with, and Mrs. Bates was carrying a tray of tea and cakes. "Hello Mrs. T., hello Mr. T.," she said, and the two older people were warm in their greetings. "Hello

Mrs Bates" Eleanor said, "How are you?" The two women carried on talking, while Deborah took her father-in-law to a seat in front of the fire, where he sat, and stroked Bouncer. The pup was behaving well, she thought to herself, and this was borne out by her father-in-law. "He's doing very well Debby" he said, "His mother doesn't miss the pups at all now she's back with Bella and us, and living in the house. So, how are things with you and Hayden? Have you heard from Rickards yet, about any progress with the case?" Deborah told him all she knew, before she went to pour out the tea, and they all sat down together to catch up on family gossip. "Maggie McKendrick saw us just yesterday, and wishes to be remembered to you" Eleanor said "She hoped she didn't upset you, when she talked to you."

"I've been trying to forget everything she said" Deborah answered quietly, "she said things that I didn't understand, but when my cousin turned up on the doorstep and Bouncer started barking and growling at him, both Hayden and I wondered if he was the little one that she referred to."

"Didn't think about that" David said, "but that could be it. He's not a big boy yet, so he might be the little one."

"People have been referring to him as a little one ever since we bought him home" Deborah said. "But I didn't think about it for a while." She smiled. "Whatever time did you start out this morning? I mean, it took Hayden and myself nearly seven hours to get here after we'd been to visit you." She told them of the storm and the crash, and was relieved when David said he knew all about it. "Were you frightened?" he asked, and she nodded. "I don't like storms anyway, and to be left in the car alone, but for Bouncer, was an experience I wouldn't like to repeat."

"We stayed overnight with Sandra and saw her and the children. The new baby is lovely, and we really enjoyed meeting him, so our journey from her home, wasn't as long" Eleanor said, and the conversation became general. Deborah was going to show her parents in law to their room, when the door opened and Hayden came in, and greeted his parents. "You managed to get off work then?" his father asked with a grin, and Hayden nodded. "There are some perks to being a consultant" he said, and the two men smiled together. Deborah knew that her father-in-law had also been a consultant surgeon before he retired to take over the estate in Scotland, and had seen that the two men were good friends as well as being father and son. The conversation carried on, and Deborah was drawn into a talk with Eleanor about clothes. She knew Hayden was listening, but was surprised when he asked his mother if she would go with her and buy a dress. "It's for the Hospital Ball" he said. "I wondered if you and Katrina would like to go with Debby and see what you can find. She's got to outshine everybody there, so she needs something grand." His mother had agreed, and as they went into dinner that evening, Deborah knew she was going to enjoy their visit.

When Katrina arrived the following day, Deborah began to enjoy herself even more. Katrina was eight years younger than her brother, but it was obvious they were very good friends, and spent time together, laughing and teasing each other. Deborah and Katrina took to each other immediately and she was drawn into the laughter, and by the end of the first day of her visit, she felt she had laughed more in one day, than in all the time since her father had passed away. She had received a letter from Mr. Rickards, telling her that the court case would be starting within the next month, and gave the date, and she should hold herself in readiness to be called as a witness. She showed the letter to Hayden, and he nodded. “I'll make sure I'll be available.” he said. “I'm not letting you go through that on your own.”

Eleanor and Katrina were entranced by the thought of going shopping for a dream dress for Deborah, and two days later, they were on the way into town. They had to change trains at one underground station, and it was as they were standing on the platform, that Deborah began to feel as though someone were watching her. She glanced around her, and became still as she saw her cousin Dudley staring at her from the opposite platform. “Are you okay Debby?” Eleanor asked her, as she saw the girl's white face and Deborah nodded. “My cousin is on the other platform, staring at me” she said. “Where?” Eleanor asked, and Deborah pointed him out. Just then, Dudley's train arrived, and when it left the station, Dudley was nowhere to be seen. “I hate him” she said, “he's a bully, and he made threats against me, when he came to Hayden's house. Bouncer didn't like him, and was growling and barking all the time he was there.” Eleanor took her hand, and held it tight. “He won't be able to hurt you, Debby. Hayden will look after you, and Mrs. Bates will make sure he doesn't gain access to the house.”

“I hope so” Deborah said with feeling, but the train arrived then, and the three women made their way to Knightsbridge station. “We're going to Harrods” Eleanor said, “That's the place to find the special dress that will help you outshine everybody”, and Katrina laughed. “Oh good” she said. “I love going there, and trying on dresses. It's going to be fun.” And it was. Deborah forgot about Dudley as she looked at dress after dress, until she saw the one she wanted. It was a deep blue satin, with long puffed sleeves, and quite a low neckline. The skirt was ruched and gathered, and when she tried it on, she realised it suited her well. “I think you'll need some jewellery to wear with that” Katrina said, but Deborah shook her head. “I don't have any” she said. “Perhaps I could buy something to wear with it?”

“But hasn't my cheapskate brother given you loads of jewellery?” she asked, and Deborah shook her head. “There's no need for him to give me anything” she said, but Katrina continued talking. “I'm going to have something to say to him” she said. “When a man marries, he should shower his wife with jewellery and stuff, if he loves her. Doesn't Hayden love you enough to do such a thing?” “Leave it Katrina” Deborah said, “Don't ask him any questions please.” she shook her head and turned to Eleanor, “I knew something like this would happen” she said bitterly to her mother-in-law. “Please will you tell her.” she turned away, “I'm going to get changed” and she walked to the changing room, where the assistant helped her to change out of the dress, and don her everyday clothes. When she walked out of the changing room, Katrina gave her a hug. “I'm sorry,” she said, “I didn't know.”, and shook her head.

"Don't you dare pity me" Deborah said quietly. "I don't want any, and I've decided I don't want the dress, because I'm not going to the Ball." She was in a temper now, and Eleanor saw it, and shook her head at her daughter. "Don't say anything" she said quietly. "And don't offer her any pity. She doesn't want it, and right now, she doesn't want anything to be said to her." Deborah had walked away from the two women, but Katrina shook her head. "Hayden's going to be spitting mad when she tells him she's not going to the Ball, and he's going to be really annoyed at me, for having bought up the subject" She sighed. "It was lovely to come and see him, but I didn't expect anything like this." She started to talk to her mother about something else, and when Deborah had regained her equilibrium, she was able to join in the conversation without any problem. Katrina had found a dress now, and gone to try it on. "It will suit her" her mother said. "She's always been able to wear that colour. Like you, you can wear most colours, but if I were you, I'd go for the deeper colours. With blonde hair, it will make a contrast against a deep colour."

"I've got quite a few darker coloured dresses now" Deborah said, "but I won't be buying any more for a long time, until I've managed to get my own funds. You've seen the letter that the solicitor wrote telling me the court case will be starting next month? With any luck, it might all be sorted by the end of January. Then I'll be able to move out of Hayden's house, and into mine. Do you reckon he would object if I took Bouncer with me? He would be company for me."

"Deborah, you don't need to move away from Hayden" Eleanor said quietly. "He cares for you, and he doesn't

want you to be too badly upset."
"I'll have to go" she said strongly, then turned away, but not before Eleanor had seen the glint of tears in her eyes. "Because you love him?" she said, and before she could stop herself, Deborah nodded. "Don't say anything to him please" she begged and Eleanor nodded, then stopped to look as her daughter came from the changing room, and smiled as she saw her. "Oh, that really suits you" she said, "I do hope you're going to, have it?" Katrina nodded, and twirled in front of the mirror. "Jeremy told me there would be quite a few things I'd have to go to this Christmas, so I'll buy it for those" she said. "And after that, I think shoes as well. What about you Mum? What do you fancy for yourself?" Eleanor smiled, "I might just have a look around for something for Christmas" she said, and Deborah pulled herself together, and went to inspect a rack of designer gowns. She noticed with regret the lovely dress she had tried on, being replaced on the rack, and turned away from the sight, and threw herself into admiring the gowns that were being paraded in front of them. At last, shopping concluded and paid for, and arranged to be delivered to Hayden's house, they went to have lunch in the restaurant, and she felt a lot calmer than she had done.

When they got home, Hayden was talking to his father, and as the three women walked in, they both stood up. "Found something nice?" he asked Deborah, and she shook her head. "I'm not going to the Ball" she said. "I've decided it's going to be much easier on you, if you don't have to explain my absence when I leave." Hayden's eyes narrowed, and his mother took

his hand. “Leave it” she hissed. “I'll explain later.” He nodded, as Deborah left the room, to go upstairs and hang her coat in the wardrobe. “Don't say a word” Eleanor said, when she had gone. “Deborah has obviously got something on her mind at the moment, and we don't want her to be too upset. Leave it for a while, but don't worry, she has got a dress to wear, I asked for it to be delivered here, so when our stuff comes, it will be with it.” Hayden sat down again, and Katrina came into the room. “I'm sorry” she said, “it was all my fault, but don't yell at me.”
“Sisters!” Hayden said. “They always upset things, don't they?” he asked his father, but the older man shook his head. “Don't say anything against your sister” he said. “She's quite nice really, and you'd miss her if she didn't come and see you occasionally.”

The evening passed quietly, and nothing was said to Deborah by Hayden to upset her, and she went to bed that evening, feeling happier than she had done, leaving Hayden talking to his parents. The parcels had been delivered that evening, and had been taken to Eleanor or Katrina's rooms. She had felt upset that she had decided that she wasn't going to the Ball, and be able to wear the fantastic dress she had chosen, but knew she was doing the right thing. If she went to the Ball with Hayden, all his colleagues would get to meet her, and when she left him, he would have to explain everything, and she didn't want him to be too disturbed. She was thinking only of Hayden, but knew he was annoyed. He didn't say anything however, and the rest of Katrina's visit was very enjoyable. She had told Hayden that she had seen Dudley, but hadn't spoken to him, and he nodded, but didn't say anything.

On the day of the Ball, however, Hayden came home early in the afternoon and found her playing with Bouncer in the garden. He came up to her, kissed her on the cheek, and said "Go and start to get ready for the Ball."
"I told you, I'm not going" she said firmly, but he shook her head.
"Oh yes, you are. I've been asked by a lot of people if you're going to be there, and I've decided that you will accompany me."
"I don't have anything to wear" she argued, but he shook his head again and grinned. "You have you know. The dress you liked, is up in Mum's bedroom, and is ready for you to wear."
"I don't want to go" she argued, but he was adamant.
"You will go to the Ball Cinderella. If necessary, I'll come and help you get dressed, and drag you there by your hair."
"You're a bully" she said angrily, and he grinned and nodded. "It will be fun" he said. "You'll enjoy yourself, and you'll meet a lot of my colleagues at the hospital. You'll even meet up with the Sister and some of the nurses who looked after you when you were a patient. They want to see you again, and see how you've got on." She sighed and capitulated. "Okay, I'll go. It would be nice to see them again."
"Good girl" he said, and kissed her cheek, and watched her walk away.

Eleanor and Katrina helped her to get ready for the Ball that evening, and as she went downstairs that evening, a fur cape around her shoulders, and holding onto a small handbag, Hayden was waiting for her. "My goodness me" he exclaimed, "you look fantastic. But that dress needs something round the neckline." and he held out a gold chain. "Wear this" he said, "it will accentuate the dress, and I promise you can give it back at the end of the day, when you don't need it anymore." Reluctantly she took it, and had a good look. It was a thick chain, and it had a large sapphire jewel drop in the centre of it. "Turn round" he instructed, and draped it around her neck. His mother looked at her, and smiled. "It looks lovely on you my dear." Deborah took a look at herself in the mirror and had to agree. It set off the neckline perfectly, and it suited her well. "Okay, let's go" he said, "See you later Mum. Give my love to Grandmother." and he escorted her out to the car.

The dinner party taking place before the Ball was held in the hospital canteen, which had been decorated, and didn't resemble a canteen at all. Deborah and Hayden were welcomed by the governors of the hospital, and greeted by other members of the hospital staff, and she enjoyed herself as they ate the meal that was served to them. When they were finished, they were all escorted into the ballroom, and Hayden took her in his arms and danced her away from the receiving line. They had been dancing for a while, and she was enjoying being held in his arms, when she glanced around the room, and saw, to her horror, her cousin Dudley and his wife, shaking hands with the treasurer of the hospital who she had been introduced to earlier. She abruptly stopped dancing, and Hayden followed her line of sight, and turned away, shielding her from his sight. "What's he doing here?" she asked. "Surely he doesn't have anything to do with the hospital?"

"No," Hayden said simply, "he doesn't. I think I'll have a chat with a couple of people. I'll take you to a room where you won't have to see him, and I'll see what I can find out." and he escorted her to one of the small rooms off the main ballroom. She sat in one of the armchairs, waiting for Hayden's return, and jumped visibly when the door opened and the Sister and the young nurse who had looked after her when she had been an inpatient, came in. "Hello Deborah" Sister Phelps said, and the young nurse with her smiled at her. "Mr. Tomlinson asked us to come and sit with you, while he makes a few enquiries, so you won't be lonely, and of course it's nice for us to be able to see you again." the Sister continued, and came to sit beside her. They carried on chatting for a while, as they asked after her health and what she had been doing since she left the hospital, she told them about Bouncer, and they were laughing as she told them about his antics, until the door opened and Hayden came in. "He's gone" he said. "Thank you, Sister, and you too Nurse Evans. I'm grateful to you both."

The two women said their farewells, and left the room, and Hayden took the chair by Deborah. "I've found out why he was here. He and his father offered the hospital a large donation, and they had accepted it, not knowing it wasn't his to give. They offered him a place here at the Ball to say thanks. I asked how much he gave and the amount made even me raise my eyebrows. But they know now, that the money isn't his

to give, so they're not going to allocate it yet in case it has to be returned, which it might have to be, if the courts decide in your favour. There's a stop on spending the money as well as transferring it from one account to another, and he can't give it away either."
"He and Uncle Arthur are trying to get rid of the money they got from my father, so he won't have to give me any" Deborah said, and Hayden nodded. "That's what I was thinking. I've just phoned Rickards and he's going to get an accountant to contact him, and remind him about the enforcement on him giving any money away. They can't do this to you."
"They're doing that already" she said bitterly, and her eyes watered. "I don't object to the money being given, because it's to a good cause, but I object to him and his father doing it to try and cheat me and my father." She wiped the tears away with her hand, and he handed her a handkerchief. "Don't cry Debby" he said, and stood up, to pull her to her feet, where he took her in his arms, and kissed her. The kiss grew longer and deeper, and she responded, kissing him back. At last, he broke the kiss and looked down into her eyes. "We'll sort him out" he said, "I promise you we will." She smiled tremulously, and he hugged her close. "Come on, let's go outside and we can have a dance." and he led her out of the room.

She had danced several times with him, before she was asked by one of the other consultants to dance with him, and Hayden allowed him to take Deborah away. Their steps didn't match so well, and she wasn't really enjoying herself, but she listened with interest to what he was saying. "Of course," he said, "your husband is a brilliant surgeon, and so young to be a professor."

"A professor?" Deborah said, and immediately regretted it for she knew what the man would say. "Didn't you know?" he asked, but she nodded. "It probably didn't register" she said. "I've had a lot of problems going on in my life lately, and when I first knew him, I'd had an accident, and I'd been suffering from a concussion." The consultant nodded, "Are you fully recovered now?" he asked and she nodded, as she continued to dance with him. After that, she was passed from consultant to consultant to dance. From time to time, she saw Hayden dancing with other women, and hoped he would soon return to partner her. She had been asked by a doctor to have a dance, and knew she recognised him from somewhere, and when he introduced himself as Jake Lovell, knew he was the registrar who had looked after her on the ward. "Hello Lady Deborah" he said, as they danced, and she smiled. "Hello Mr. Lovell. How are you these days?"

"Busy" he replied laconically, "your husband is a glutton for work, and he keeps me busy." she laughed at that, for she couldn't imagine that Hayden would work so hard, for he always appeared to be so laid back. "Mind you," he said, "he's a damn good surgeon, and I can understand why they wanted him to be knighted." Deborah felt a cold shiver run down her back, and couldn't say very much. She needed to process what he had said, and decided to ignore it. "I wanted to thank you for looking after me when I wasn't well" she said and he grinned. "Just doing my job" he said. "Mind you, it was a bit disconcerting to be told what to give you and how to treat you, by your new boss, when you had no idea who he was."

"Hadn't you even met him?" she asked, and he shook his head. "We knew he'd been appointed, but not many people had met him, and I certainly had no idea who my new boss was. I was taken on one side by Sister Phelps, and she informed me that I was to obey every order given to me by him, because he knew a hell of a lot more about the patient than I did." He smiled at her. "When did you get married? Nobody seems to know."

"A couple of weeks after I was discharged from hospital." she said with a smile, but before Jake could ask her more questions, thankfully the music finished, and he escorted her to rejoin Hayden. The band were having a break, so everybody was having a rest from the dancing. She didn't say anything to him, about the things she had been told, and he took her into the dining room, where the tables had been set for drinks and nibbles. "After the meal we had, I don't want anything else" she said, and he smiled. "Well come and have a drink instead" and he led her to the counter. "So, what do you want?" he asked, and she opted for a glass of wine. They were standing apart from other people, when the treasurer of the hospital came to talk to them. "Mrs. Tomlinson, I wanted to have a word with you, if you wouldn't mind. It's about the donation your cousin made to the hospital," and he told her the amount he had given. "I understand from your husband that your relatives aren't entitled to any of the money he is giving away, and the money is subject to a court case?" Deborah nodded, and made sure that nobody else was in earshot. "I don't know if my husband has told you what's happened?" she said softly, and the treasurer nodded. "I don't object to the hospital being given the donation, especially as it's such a good cause, but the amount is such that it might be everything that I'm owed. However, what I will object to, is if my cousin and my uncle get credited with giving the money. I would prefer that if there is any credit to be given, then it be given to my father" The man nodded, and smiled at her. "We don't actually know if we would be able to accept it yet" he said, "as the money is subject to a court case, but might I assure you that if we do so, then it would be credited to your father, and definitely not your uncle or your cousin. Might I ask you if you would keep us up to date with the court's decisions?" he asked, and she nodded. "You'll probably see it in the papers" she said. "I don't think it's going to be kept out of the public eye."

"If you do decide to let us have some money, it will be very gratefully received" he said, and they discussed the use the donation would be put to. "You have our deepest sympathy" he said, "on what's been happening to you and on the loss of your father. I knew him from work he did on my own home." He shook her hand, and took his leave and Hayden looked at her, as they stood together. "Do you want to go home?" he asked, but she shook her head. "No, I think I've had enough shocks this evening, there surely can't be many more, so we might as well stay and I can enjoy the dancing."

"What other shocks have you had?" he laughed at her, but she shook her head. "Dudley for a start", she said. "Oh Hayden, why does he have to be at the same places as I am. I told you I saw him on the underground platform when I was going to Harrods, and I felt uneasy all day. I was quite happy this evening, and then I saw him. Every time I see him, I feel dirty, and as if he's going to do something that will hurt me, despite the fact that he's never physically abused me, just held me down for his father to hit me. He is just such an obnoxious man, obviously got that, from his father."

"Your uncle wasn't your father's brother?" he asked, and she shook her head. "No, we're related through my mother. She was the sister of Aunt Claudia. But Mum was so different to her sister. I miss her so much, which is why I think I relate so well to your mother. Maybe I just need another mother figure." She laughed, "which is stupid when you think about it."

"It's not stupid at all. It's quite well known that girls need their mothers more from their late teens to their early twenties. You're still in that group, don't forget, and it's natural that you'd miss your mother." She sighed, and Hayden looked at her downcast head. "Don't fret Debby" he said, "next month, we'll be going to court and things will start to make sense. You'll be fine, I know you will." They took their drinks outside to their table, and when the music started again, he swept her onto the dance floor, and they danced several times. She was passed to other people after that, and when the music began to change, to more modern music, Hayden asked her again if she would like to go, and this time, she nodded. "I think so" she said. "I'm quite tired now, and you've got to go back to work tomorrow morning."

He shook his head, "I've got the morning off

tomorrow" he laughed. "Rank has its privileges, after all." She collected her cape, and said good bye to several people, and Hayden took her out to the car. The drive home was soon achieved, and she waited while Hayden put the car into the garage, before they went into the front door. "Come and have some coffee" he invited. "Mrs. Bates always leaves some on the stove for me, in case I get called out at night" and he led her into the kitchen. Bouncer was asleep in his crate, but when they went into the kitchen, he woke up, and wanted to be petted, so Hayden let him run free around the kitchen. He poured out the drink, and they sat together, not talking much, as they drank it. She had drunk half her drink, when she looked at him, and said, "Why didn't you tell me you'd been knighted?" He looked surprised, then resigned, "Who talked?" he asked, and she grinned. "Jake Lovell" she said. "We were dancing, and he told me then. Wasn't he meant to say anything?" Hayden shook his head, and emboldened, she said, "and the professorship? What about that then? And that wasn't Jake. He didn't say anything about that. But when we were talking about your job last week, you never said a word! So, when did you get the knighthood?"

"About four years ago" he said. "I developed some instruments that made the job a bit easier than it had been, and my colleagues seemed to agree, and the next thing I got a letter from the PM's office asking if I would be willing to accept an honour from the Queen. She was very nice to talk to when I went to collect the award. Mum liked it as well, because she and Dad came with me."

"And what about the professorship? When did you get

that?"
"Just before I started here." he answered. "I told you I had to do more studying; well, those were the exams for the job at the hospital. I heard I'd passed the exams on the same day I got the job," he grinned at the expression on her face. "Am I forgiven for keeping it a secret?" he asked, and she smiled and nodded. "Did everybody agree to keep it a secret?" she asked, and he nodded. "I did ask everybody not to say anything, but obviously Jake forgot."
"He called me Lady Deborah, and I thought he was being polite, until he mentioned the knighthood. He said he only found out who you were when I was taken in to the ward, and you told him what to do." He smiled at the memory. "He's a damn good surgeon, and when he gets a bit more experience, I'm going to have to watch my back. But don't you dare tell him I said that" he said fiercely. She drank the remains of her coffee and stood up. "When will I ever have the opportunity to tell him?" she asked. "I doubt I'll ever meet him again." She put her empty mug into the sink. "I think I'd better go to bed." she reached up and took the necklace off, and handed it to him. "Thank you for letting me borrow it" she said, and swiftly went out of the room.
Hayden watched her go, before he put his mug into the sink, picked up the necklace, urged Bouncer back into his crate, and shut the door on the puppy, before following Deborah up the stairs to go to his bed.

Chapter Nine

"The judgement of this court is that all monies in the account of Mr. Robert Andrew Parkes, at the time of his death, are to be paid to his daughter, Miss Deborah Ellen Parkes, now known as Lady Deborah Ellen Tomlinson. All monies to be paid immediately to Lady Deborah Tomlinson. The house, address 15 Deventer Drive, was taken fraudulently by Mr. Arthur Cummins, and its ownership will revert immediately to Lady Deborah Tomlinson, and Mr. and Mrs. Cummins must vacate the premises without any further delay. The business of Parkes Builders which was the property of Mr. Robert Parkes, and which has been taken over by Mr. Arthur Cummins, must revert to Lady Deborah Tomlinson, and the monies in the bank account of the company at the time of his decease, should be paid back to Lady Deborah." The judge stopped to take a breath, and continued. "I understand that the police will be questioning Mr. Arthur Cummins and Mr. Dudley Cummins over the fraudulent way that the monies were removed from the control of Lady Deborah Tomlinson, and they are facing further charges regarding the assaults on Lady Deborah. In addition, the way that Mr. Dudley Cummins acted is strictly against the edict of the Law Society, and he will be referred to the society for disciplinary action. Sentencing will be delayed for three weeks." The judge stopped talking, and Deborah felt her knees go weak. Hayden gave her hand a squeeze, and she could see her mother- and father-in-law sitting nearby, smiling at her. Her uncle and cousin were glaring at her, and she knew that the enmity that had been present, was now increased tenfold. She shivered, and Hayden put his arm around her, and gave her a hug. "What's the problem?" he asked, "You won" She nodded, and said quietly, "Look at my uncle's face. He's going to try and get his own back and I'm worried what he's going to do."

"Don't fret sweetheart" he said. "The police will make sure that they are kept away from you, and he won't be able to hurt you. I promise you that." She felt safe in his presence, but knew that he would not be able to be with her all the time, and knew that she would have to make her own way in the world in the not-too-distant future. The trial had lasted nearly two weeks, and her uncle had done his best to persuade the judge that her father had wanted him to have everything, and Dudley had put forward the papers he said her father had signed, but they had been discounted, by the graphologist, and the whole case had collapsed after that, for her lawyers were good and they hadn't succeeded. Her lawyers and Mr. Rickards were approaching her now, smiling, and she allowed her features to break into a smile in return, as they came to talk to her. The past couple of weeks had been very upsetting to her, and she hoped she would be able to have a break from all worry for a short while. Christmas had come and gone, and their celebrations had been muted by the approaching court case, but she had enjoyed herself all the same. They had gone to a few dinner parties given by Hayden's colleagues at the hospital, and she knew that they liked her for herself. She knew also they were very curious as to the court case which was going to start after the festive season, and had wondered what they would say if she were to lose. Hayden had given her a delicate gold watch for her present, and she wondered what he had thought of the simple gold cuff links she had given him in return. She pulled herself together now, and went to talk to Eleanor and David, who had come down from Scotland to be with her, to be at court with her and to hear the verdict. They had said they would wait until things had been settled before returning home, and she was grateful to them. Now, Hayden approached her and took her hand. "The police have just arrested your uncle and your cousin" he said softly to her. "I should imagine they will let you know what they decide to do. They'll be charged with fraud I suspect, but that doesn't carry a mandatory jail sentence, so I expect they'll be released on bail until the trial about the assaults, and then the fraud trial, all of which you'll have to attend I'm afraid. But don't fret Debby, I'll be with you." He squeezed her hand, and turned to his parents. "Come on, let's get out of here, and go and have a celebratory coffee." and he led the way from the court room.

Two weeks later, Deborah was in the car, with Bouncer in the back, and Hayden was driving to her house. The solicitor had given her a set of keys for the house, with the advice that it would probably be a good idea to have the locks changed, as soon as her aunt and uncle had arranged for their furniture to be removed. Today was the day they were going to go, and Hayden had told her that it would be a good idea to make sure they didn't take anything of hers with them, so today, they were going to do just that. He parked outside the house, and she let herself in with the key that she had been given, and gave Hayden a grin as she did so. Her aunt was in the hallway, and her smile faded as she looked at the woman. There was very little furniture left in the rooms, for they had got rid of most of her parent's belongings. Bouncer growled at her aunt, and she hushed him quickly. "What are you here for?" the other woman demanded, and Hayden smiled – not a friendly smile, and her aunt seemed to realise what a stupid question that was. "We've come to make sure that you don't take anything else of Debby's" he said. "Deborah, would you make sure that what remains of your parents' furniture is still here." She nodded, and went to check. The things that had been left behind when her aunt and uncle moved in, and hadn't got rid of, were still there, and she went back to the sitting room where Hayden and her aunt were stood face to face. "Just one thing" she said. "I'd like my mother's jewellery returned please." Hayden looked at her, and she remembered she hadn't told him she was going to ask for its return. "I don't have it. We couldn't find it." her aunt spat the words out. "Believe me, if I'd found it, I've have worn it" Deborah knew that to be true, for her aunt would have delighted in flaunting it, if she'd had the jewels. "We couldn't find it when we moved in, so I think your beloved father must have sold it before he died."

"I don't believe you" Deborah said, "Dad would never have done that. There were pieces in mother's collection that belonged to his mother and he would never have sold family pieces."

"Well, I certainly haven't got it." Her aunt spoke with

certainty now, and Hayden took her hand in his. “Leave it Debby” he said quietly. “If everything is okay, then your aunt can go.”
“As long as she hands over all the keys to the cupboards in the kitchen, which are still locked. I want to make sure she hasn't taken any of granny's China and glassware which was left to my mother.” Hayden held out his hand, and the other woman reluctantly handed over a bunch of keys, which Deborah took, and went into the kitchen. Bouncer followed her, and she spent some time checking the contents of the cupboards, for the China was old and valuable. “I can't see anything else she might have purloined” she said on her return, and Hayden nodded. “Okay, you can go” he ordered her aunt. “I don't want to hear that you've ever been seen near this house again.”
“You always were a wilful child” her aunt said to Deborah. “You could have had a good life if you'd let us carry on as we were, and not got involved with him” and she gestured to Hayden. Deborah drew in a deep breath. “A good life!” she repeated incredulously. “Acting as your unpaid servant, having to do all the cooking, cleaning and washing, not being given enough food to eat, having to do all uncle’s secretarial work, and all for a wage that was little more than pocket money, while you and Uncle lived very well in <u>my</u> house, on the money that my father had worked all his life to earn, while your husband took control of father's company! I don't think so! Just go, Aunt Claudia. Mother would have been disgusted with you. For once, I'm glad she's gone and can't see how badly you've acted and treated me. I hope I never have to see you or any other member of your family again.”

"You might not believe it now Deborah, but I did try and talk your uncle out of what he was doing" she said, but Deborah didn't believe her. "I think it's time you went" she said, and watched as the woman gathered her coat around her, and shut the door behind her. When they heard the car leave, Deborah sagged against Hayden. "I don't believe that she tried to talk Uncle Arthur out of doing what he did." she said, and was grateful for his firm arm around her. "Nor do I. But the locksmith will be coming in a few minutes" he said, "so we'll make sure that they can't gain access again. When he's been, we can go home and have lunch. Where did Bouncer go to?" Deborah looked around her, and sighed, "I don't know. I'll bet he's found something he shouldn't have done." and she went to have a look. Bouncer was curled up in front of the oven, which had been left on, and he was obviously nice and warm. "She's turned on all the fires" Hayden said, as he entered the kitchen. "She turned the oven on as well. I'll bet she thought she could try and burn the house down or something like that." Hayden shook his head. "No, but I don't think they will have paid the gas bill, and this is the last attempt on her part to make you pay for their extravagances." They went round the house, turning everything off, and Deborah was telling him about the house, when the doorbell rang, and the locksmith arrived. Once the new locks were in position, they were able to leave, and Deborah gave the house a last look as they drove away. Soon she would be installed in it again, hopefully with Bouncer as a companion, and she would be away from Hayden for good, and felt very sad as she thought about it. Hayden gave her hand a squeeze as they drew up outside his house, and he let her and the dog out. “I'd better go into the hospital,” he said. “I said I'd be back in this morning, just to see that everything is okay. I'll be home later on tonight.” and he smiled at her. She smiled back, and went inside with Bouncer. Mrs. Bates was out shopping, and so she went upstairs, with Bouncer as her companion, and into her bedroom. She opened the wardrobe door, and started to look through her wardrobe, wondering whether she ought to take everything with her for she hadn't paid Hayden back for any of them. She heard Mrs. Bates come in, and she and Bouncer went back downstairs again. “Everything okay?” the housekeeper asked, and she nodded. “My aunt and uncle have moved out, and the house is now empty of their possessions. The locks have been changed, so it should be secure now. I've got to start thinking about getting some furniture for it now, because they got rid of a lot of my father's stuff, and it's a bit bare. But I can afford it now” she said with a tremulous smile, and turned away so Mrs. Bates wouldn't see the tears that had started in her eyes. “Don't make decisions too quickly my dear” she said. “Leave it for a bit, and you can make a decision when you feel happier. Now, would you like coffee?”

“Yes please Mrs. Bates, but I'll come and make it, and you have one too. I'm sorry I wasn't able to do the shopping for you.”

“That is my job, my dear” the housekeeper smiled at her, as they went into the kitchen together, Bouncer at their heels. “That little dog is doing so well now, isn't he? He's getting so obedient.” Mrs. Bates said. “I saw Mrs. Little this morning, and she was saying she thought he'd grown incredibly since she last saw him.”

"He is getting bigger. And he's got all his adult teeth now. He was play biting Hayden this morning, and he said his teeth are incredibly sharp. He'll have to stop letting him do that. It would be awful if he wasn't able to operate because the dog had bitten him." The two women laughed together, and when Deborah had made their coffee, they sat together at the kitchen table, drinking it. That afternoon, she took Bouncer for a walk, and went to say hello to Mrs. Little, to show her the progress she was making with her knitting. "Come and see me again sometime" said the woman as they were leaving the shop, and she walked along the road, feeling quite happy, until Bouncer started growling, and she looked up to see her uncle standing on the pavement in front of her. He stared at her for a long while, but didn't say anything, and eventually just turned and walked away. When Hayden came home that evening, she told him she had seen him. "Did he do anything to hurt you?" was his question, and she shook her head. "No, he didn't even speak, just stared at me for ages, while Bouncer was growling at him, then he turned and walked away" she sighed. "I can't help it, every time I see him, I feel as though I should be wearing an apron again, and going to get his dinner ready." Hayden laughed, and took her hand. "You've got no cause to feel like that," he said, "you're free from him, He's going to have to repay all the money he took from you, so be strong Debby. He can't hurt you anymore."

"I hope so" she said, then the subject was dropped. She went to bed that evening, feeling happier than she had done for a long time, but she still had the nagging doubt that Hayden wasn't taking her uncle's threats as seriously as he could have done.

The following day, they were meant to be going out to dinner to one of Hayden's colleagues, and she occupied herself with some shopping in the morning, and arranged some flowers for the rooms. She knew she was going to have to leave Hayden very soon now, when she received the money, she was due, and the thought hurt her so badly. He was always careful of her, he would kiss her on the cheek before she went to bed in the evenings, or when he left for work in the morning, but the memory of how he had kissed her when they had been at the hospital ball, stayed with her, and she wished he would kiss her again like that for she had felt very wanted at the time. She had eaten a delicious lunch with Mrs. Bates, and she looked at Bouncer. He was living up to his name, tearing round the kitchen like a whirlwind, and she knew he needed more exercise. "I'll take him for another walk in the park and try and wear him out, although he's got so much more energy now, he's older." she told the housekeeper. "I'll have plenty of time to get ready for tonight, when I get back. We shouldn't be more than an hour" She attached the lead to his harness, and led him along the road. He was a good puppy, and obedient to her now, and they stayed out for quite a while, as he ran to and fro, chasing his ball. In the end, she looked around her, and realised they had walked quite a way from the house, and in fact were near her own house, so she called Bouncer to her, clipped his lead on, and turned to walk home, surprised that there didn't seem to be very many people around, when Bouncer suddenly started growling. "What's the problem Bouncer?" she asked, bending to stroke his head, when she saw her uncle and cousin approaching her swiftly. She turned away, wanting to get away from them, but she wasn't fast enough, and felt a sharp pain in her head, and knew her uncle or her cousin had hit her. Her head felt odd somehow, but she could hear that Bouncer was barking loudly, and she felt as if she couldn't move properly, felt hard hands on her arms, and was half walked, half dragged, by both men towards her house. "Where are the keys?" she was asked, and knowing she couldn't fight them both, she pulled out the set of keys from her pocket. Bouncer was barking loudly, and growling at them both, and her vision was fuzzy, but she saw her cousin kick the small dog, and herd him yelp in pain, then she felt the lead, which she had looped over her wrist become limp, and saw Bouncer run away. The door of her house was opened, and she was marched inside. Her vision cleared slightly, and she saw her cousin's fist raise, and felt a sharp pain again. She could feel something damp on the side of her head, and knew she was bleeding again. "You bitch" Dudley snarled at her. "You ungrateful little bitch. You couldn't be happy letting us look after your affairs, could you? Had to run away and get sympathy from that doctor. And then the hospital wouldn't accept the donation we were going to make them, because you and your husband had told them it wasn't ours to give."

"Well, it isn't" she started to argue, and felt her uncle hit her again, on the same place as before, and she felt the blood flow freely. "Let me go, and we'll say nothing more about it." Her uncle gave a short laugh. "Don't be stupid." he said. "You're going to disappear

completely now, and the will you make will give us back everything, all the money, this house and the company."
"My will is lodged with my solicitor. Everything goes to my husband" she argued, her head aching where her uncle had hit her, but he laughed. "No, you're going to make another one right now." and he pulled her into the kitchen. Dudley was holding her tight, so she couldn't escape, and her uncle took her left hand in both of his, slowly twisted her wrist in both of his, and her eyes filled with tears. Her uncle laughed at her expression, then started to bend her fingers back one at a time. The pain was incredible, lancing up her arm, and she screamed, and saw her uncle smile evilly at her pain. "Write this down" he said, and produced a will form, and a piece of paper. "Copy that, then sign it" he ordered, twisting her wrist viciously again, and she knew he had no intention of letting her go, and she had no alternative. When she hesitated, he started to bend her fingers back again, and she knew he would break them if she fought. "Write it, bitch" He hit her on the side of the head again, and she staggered, as she wiped the blood out of her eyes, picked up the pen, and started to write. When it came to the signature, she signed it Deborah Elaine Parkes, and hoped they wouldn't notice, for her middle name was Ellen, and not Elaine, and she had used her maiden name and not her married name. Eventually it was done, glanced at by her uncle, and he nodded with a nasty smile on his face. "Now get rid of her" her uncle ordered, and her cousin dragged her along the hallway, and she wondered where they were going to take her. However, he opened the door of the cupboard under

the stairs, and she saw with horror that the trapdoor to the cellar was open, and knew where they were going to put her. She had always hated the cellar, and had as little to do with it as possible, never going down there if she could help it. “No, please no” she gasped, but her relatives took no notice. Her uncle dragged her to the top of the staircase, then put his hand in the middle of her back and pushed her down the stairs, and she stumbled on them, missed a step and fell, landing in a heap at the bottom of the staircase. Her uncle came down the stairs after her, stood beside her and smirked. “You think we were starving you when you lived with us?” he said, “You're going to find out now what starvation is really like” he said, and he kicked her, the blow landing on the side of her head. “Goodbye dear niece” then he had gone up the stairs, and the light was turned off as the cellar door was closed, and she could hear it being bolted. “Let me out” she yelled, aware that they were leaving her, and she knew she was alone. She tried to stand, then heard the front door slam, and she sank back to sit on the floor of the cellar, and sobbed. “Oh Hayden, Hayden, please come and help me” she begged, then her headache got worse, and she knew she didn't feel very well at all. She could feel her head spinning, and she fell backwards as everything went black.

Ninety minutes after Deborah had left, Mrs Bates could hear Bouncer barking frantically at the front door and went to open it. Mrs. Tomlinson had obviously forgotten her keys, she thought, and opened the door, to admit the little dog. His lead was trailing after him, and he was barking fit to burst. She peered around the door, anxious to see Deborah, but there was no sign of her. "Where's your mum?" she asked the dog, and bent to pick him up. He yelped in pain as she did so, and her worry grew. She shut the front door, and took the dog into the kitchen. He was still barking, and as she tried to take his harness off, she noticed that the loop of the lead was missing, and the end looked as though it had been cut. She knew there was something wrong now, and picked up the phone, dialled, and was soon connected with Hayden. "Oh, Sir Hayden, I'm sorry, but I'm that worried" she began. "Mrs. T. took Bouncer out for a walk nearly two hours ago, and he's just come home without her. He's got an injury on his side, looks like he's been kicked, and his lead doesn't have a loop on it. Mrs. T. always loops it over her wrist, and it looks like it's been cut. What shall I do?" Hayden was sitting at his desk, going over patients notes, but now he pushed them aside, and stood up. "Do nothing Mrs. Bates. I'm on my way home, and I'll be with you shortly." and he put the phone down, told his secretary he was going home, and was soon on his way. When he let himself in the house, he went straight to the kitchen. Bouncer was still shivering, held in the housekeeper's arms, but when he saw Hayden, he barked again. "No sign of Debby?" he asked, and the housekeeper shook her head. "Nothing" she said. "Oh Mr. T., what's happened to her?"

"I don't know" he said, "But I've got a bad feeling about this. Where did she say she was going?"

"She said she was going to take him to the park to try and wear him out" she answered "But I don't know how far she would walk. She took his ball so she was

going to let him off his lead."
"Let me see him" he said, and took the puppy from her. When he touched the dog's side, it yelped, and he carefully felt it. Bouncer growled, and Hayden knew that the little dog was in pain. "I'm sure he's been kicked" he said. "I'm going to go and look for her. In the meantime, can you phone the police? They know that they're meant to be keeping a good eye on her, after the threats from her uncle and cousin." he stopped suddenly "Bouncer where's your mum?" he asked, and the puppy wriggled out of his arms, and went to the door, barking loudly. "I think he knows" he said softly. "Tell the police to meet me at her house. Where's Bouncer's spare lead?" and when it was produced, he clipped it to the harness, and opened the door. The dog pulled him to the front door and stood barking, until he could open it.

The journey to Deborah's house was achieved swiftly, and Hayden couldn't believe how quickly the little dog was pulling him along. He continued to encourage the puppy. He said, "find mum, Bouncer", and they were soon at the road where Debby's house stood. A police car was waiting for him, and the constable got out now. "Do you know if she's in there?" he asked, and Hayden nodded. "I think she's inside" he said. "I've got a key" and he took the key he had taken from the locksmith from his pocket. The policeman said, "Ready?" and drew his stick, as he opened the door. Bouncer rushed in and stood barking in the hallway. There was no sound at all, apart from the dog barking, and Hayden went swiftly into all the rooms downstairs, but there was no sign of Debby. He went upstairs, checked all the bedrooms but found no sign of her, and the policeman coming upstairs met him. “No sign of her at all downstairs.” he said. “What about the attic?” he asked, and Hayden saw the hatch above him. The policeman picked up the opener, which was propped against the wall, and opened the hatch, and got the ladder down, Hayden ran up it to look, but there was no sign of Debby there. He saw a small box on the floor hidden behind a roof truss, labelled “For Debby” and opened it and gasped, as he saw it was full of jewellery, Deborah's mothers’ jewels. He put the lid back on and they went downstairs again, and Hayden gasped, as he saw an object on the floor. “That's the loop of Bouncers lead” he said “She was here. Oh Deb, my darling Debby, where are you?” Bouncer was still standing in front of the cupboard door, and barking fit to burst, and the policeman opened the cupboard door, and the dog rushed in. He was standing on the cellar trap door, barking loudly, and Hayden hushed him. He saw the bolt – a new one – on the trap door, and noted the padlock attached to it. He and the policeman exchanged glances, and carefully the policeman took the screwdriver he found on the floor, and levered the entire padlock out of the floor. He pulled the bolt back, opened the cellar door, and Bouncer ran down the stairs. The policeman located the light switch, and Hayden looked down and saw a crumpled form on the floor, with Bouncer standing beside it, nosing it gently. “Call for an ambulance” he called as he ran down the cellar stairs, and found Deborah lying where she had fallen. Carefully now, he felt her arms and legs, found she didn't seem to be injured there, and felt her head. His fingers came away bloodstained, and his face became still. He took a deep breath and started to examine her more thoroughly. She groaned, and her eyelids fluttered. "Debby" he said, "Debby my darling, I'm here." She groaned again, "My head hurts" she said. "I called you and you came. And Bouncer's here as well" Her voice grew fainter. "Oh Hayden, I do love you" she said, then she stopped talking and her head flopped against his chest. "Debby!" Hayden said loudly, and felt for a pulse. It was there, faint and irregular, and he was frowning as he kissed her forehead. Bouncer was whimpering, as he nosed Deborah, and he put out a hand and soothed the little dog, then soon there were sirens and noises, and the ambulance crew arrived.

When Deborah awoke, she recognised the room as the one she had occupied previously, and saw as she had done before, Hayden, but this time he was sitting on the side of the bed, holding her hand, and she tried to lift her head from the pillow, but it hurt, and she lay back against the pillow. "Oh, my darling girl, you're awake at last" he said, bending his head to kiss her forehead. "How do you feel?"
"As though I've gone ten rounds with Mike Tyson" she whispered. "My head hurts, my face is sore, and I can't remember how I got here."
"You've got another concussion, but I don't think there's any lasting harm" he said. "You've been unconscious for quite a while. Do you remember meeting your uncle this afternoon?" he asked softly, and her eyes opened wide as memory of that afternoon came rushing back. "Yes," she said slowly. "He and Dudley forced me to go with them to my

house, he made me write a new will, then they locked me in the cellar, and told me I'd find out what starvation was really like. Then they left the house, and I think I must have passed out, because my head hurt really badly. He'd kicked me in the head as well, and that was really painful." Hayden frowned. "How did he make you write a new will?" he asked, and she indicated her wrist. "He was bending my fingers back, and twisting my wrist. I thought he was going to break my wrist, or my fingers. It was so sore, and he kept hitting me as well, where he'd made me bleed before, and that made it worse. I had to copy what he'd written onto a new will form, and then sign it. He said that I was going to give them back the money they'd had to give me." Hayden picked up her wrist and saw the bruising on it, noted too, the bruising on the fingers and his face darkened. "Where's my wedding ring?" she asked, for it had been removed from her finger. "It's here" he said, and she saw it in his hand. "They took it off, when they saw your fingers were bruised." She nodded, for she didn't want to lose the ring, for she treasured it, but then wanted to know everything. "How did you know where I was?" she asked him, and he smiled. "It was Bouncer. You hadn't returned from your walk, and Bouncer ran back to the house, Mrs. Bates found him on the doorstep, saw the lead they'd cut, and got worried. She phoned me and I went home, collected Bouncer and he practically dragged me to the house. When I saw you lying on the cellar floor, I thought you were dead." he groaned, and she put her hand to his face. "Not yet" she said. "A bit battered, but I'm alright really" He gathered her into his arms, held her close and kissed her gently, and she looked at him, her eyes open wide. "What was that for?" she asked and he smiled gently at her, "I love you Debby, I've loved you from the first time I saw you," he said softly, "and as you told me you love me, I think we ought to do something about that, don't you?" and he kissed her again, not at all gently this time, and when he lifted his head, she was gasping. "When did I tell you I loved you?" she asked, when she got some breath back. "When I found you in the cellar, you told me you'd called me and I'd come for you, and you told me that you loved me. And then you passed out on me and until I took your pulse, I thought you were dead. You scared the living daylights out of me, I can tell you." She reached up to kiss him again, and he held her tight against him. "Oh Hayden, I love you so much" she muttered. Her arms were around his neck, and he was holding her tightly, kissing her, deep passionate kisses, which she was returning, when the door opened, and Jake Lovell and Sister Phelps walked in. "Oh sorry" Sister mumbled, in embarrassment but Jake just grinned at his boss. "I see she's awake" he said. "Can she remember everything?" Hayden nodded and released her and Deborah laid back against the pillows. "Why don't you ask me?" she said, and he went red. "Sorry Lady Deborah." he said. "How do you feel now?" She smiled at him. "Very happy, apart from a headache and various aches and pains. Did you have to stitch my head up again?" she asked and Hayden shook his head. "I got one of the plastic surgeons do it," he said with a grin. "I couldn't, because my hands were shaking so much. You were still unconscious at that point." He smiled at her. "You've got to stop getting beaten up like this. It's not doing my nerves any good whatsoever." He turned to Sister. "I'll let you do her observations" he said, "but I think she'll be okay now, and I can take her home soon. All the scans and X rays are clear. At least this time, we won't have to deal with her uncle trying to drag her out of the bed, and take her away." The ward sister nodded, and Deborah held her wrist out, so her pulse could be taken. "What's going to happen to him?" Deborah asked, and was aware that Hayden's face was grim. "One of your neighbours saw him and your cousin dragging you into the house, and told me when we were waiting for the ambulance to come. They have both been arrested on kidnap charges, unlawful imprisonment and grievous bodily harm. They won't be allowed out as they're still on bail from the forgery and fraud charges." Deborah sighed as she moved her head, and felt the headache return. "Get some sleep my darling" he said. "I'll be here when you wake up" and he kissed her gently on the forehead, before leaving the room with Jake. "Do you want anything to drink Deborah?" asked the Sister but she shook her head, and winced. "No, I think I ought to do what Hayden said, and get some sleep, and hopefully this headache will go while I'm asleep." Sister Phelps smiled. "I think it will" she said. And she allowed Deborah to go back to sleep.

Two weeks later, she opened her eyes as she woke, and knew she was lying in Hayden's embrace, his arms tight around her, as he kissed her gently. The kiss lengthened and deepened, and she looked up into his eyes, and saw the love shining out from them. "Good morning, Debby" he said softly, as their lips parted, and she smiled at him. "Hello my darling" she whispered, and they kissed again, and his hands touched her intimately. She gasped and gave herself up to the magic of his love making. Afterwards, she lay drowsily against the pillows, and watched her husband as he came back from the shower and started to dress ready for work. She had been kept in hospital for three days until she had recovered sufficiently, and felt more like her old self, and when she had returned home, Hayden had been so good to her, giving her all the time she needed to recover fully, before they consummated their marriage. She had been astounded he could make her feel as she did, and she loved him more than ever. He could hear Bouncer barking outside the door, and he opened it, to allow the dog entry. Bouncer jumped up on the bed, and came to lie beside her. Deborah stroked the soft fur, aware of what she owed the little dog. "I think Mrs. McKendrick did mean Bouncer when she talked about the Little One." she said. "She got everything else right as well, telling me she saw happiness but trouble, and she said the ecstasy would be delayed but it would come, and believe me, it has. Thank you so much." Hayden came to take her hand, and kissed her gently. "I'm the one who should be thanking you" he said, "I love you so very much, and you've made my life better than it is already. And when the White Lady showed up, I knew the puppy was going to help you. After all, you only saw her when you were with Bouncer."

"That little lady I saw was the White Lady?" she said, her eyes open wide, and he nodded. "The stories say that she once worked in the house, when she was an old lady, and became very attached to a new member of the family, and knew when there was going to be trouble. Believe me darling, you're a very welcome addition to our family, and the rest of my family are going to love you when we all finally manage to get together. And of course, Bouncer will be with us." He bent his head to kiss her gently, and the little dog barked in agreement.

THE END

Printed in Great Britain
by Amazon

61106301R00097